Triple Crown Publications
presents

Dime Piece

by

Tracy Brown

This is a work of fiction. The authors have invented the characters. Any resemblance to actual persons, living or dead, is purely coincidental.

If you have purchased this book with a 'dull' or missing cover---You have possibly purchased an unauthorized or stolen book. Please immediately contact the publisher advising where, when and how you purchased this book.

Compilation and Introduction copyright © 2004 by
Triple Crown Publications
2959 Stelzer Road Suite C
Columbus, Ohio 43219
www.TripleCrownPublications.com

Library of Congress Control Number: 2004102061
ISBN# 0-9747895-7-7
Cover Design/Graphics: ApolloPixel.com
Editor: Kathleen Jackson
Consulting: Vickie M. Stringer

First Trade Paperback Edition Printing April 2004

Printed in the United States of America

Dedications

This book is dedicated to the women who are my sisters, though not by blood. Often, women tear each other down rather than build each other up. I consider myself blessed to have the following women in my life who have never wavered, never faltered.

Tanara Brown, My friend since nursery school. You've been in my corner since before I could read books. Now that I'm writing books, you're still the same friend. Nothing has changed, and I love you for that! Thank you for helping me navigate the countless bad situations I found myself in over the years and for sharing with me the happiness that came after the storm. You'll always be my best friend.

To Angelique Poole. You are the realest chick I know. Never fake, never phony, always a straight shooter. Thanks for being a positive friend and for motivating me when I was weary. I wish I had known you a long time ago, since the advice you give is always on point and your outlook on life shows just how much wisdom you possess. You are a great mother, a wonderful sister and an even better friend. You make me laugh every time we speak and whenever I answer the phone and hear your voice on the other end, my day seems brighter. I look forward to us being old ladies together, laughing, and drinking and reminiscing on all these memories. Save me a spot on the comfy, girl.

And last but certainly not least,, to Mosezetta F. Overby. It is difficult to label the relationship we share. You are my mom, my conscience, my confidante, my role model and most of all, my friend. You are such a beautiful person, inside and out. It's rare that one comes across a person as unselfish and genuine as you. You know what I'm thinking before I say a word, because you know me so well. You've been so supportive and so proud of my accomplishments. But more importantly, you were there <u>before</u> these accomplishments and you supported me before my feet were planted firmly. Now that I am beginning to steady myself and stand on my own two feet as a proud, independent Black woman, I salute you as the greatest example of grace and style. You are a class act. I will never forget the love you've shown me and the things you've taught me. I will never take you for granted. Let's keep praying for each other and supporting one another through good times and bad. I love you! Don't ever change.

Acknowledgments

To my family, particularly to my parents and my siblings, thank you all for rallying around me and supporting my dream. It feels good to know that I have your love and encouragement as I pursue my goals. You make it all worthwhile. To my children, Ashley, Quaviel and Justin, I love you guys and I hope you see me getting my hustle on so that you can reap the rewards. Watch and learn so that when the torch is passed to you, you can run this race and not get weary.

To my favorite legal eagles, Harvey Newkirk, Willie Dennis and Shawn Brown for your legal advice and input. Thanks for being so gracious with your time to assist me in making the decisions that are best for my career. I am forever grateful to each of you!

To my dear friend and business associate Arthur Smith, thanks for your priceless advice, your uncanny sarcasm and your ability to listen. You have a brilliant business mind, and a true hustler's spirit. I hope to go far with you on my team and I am grateful for all of your help. Thanks for getting up early to get me to venues (no matter how much you complained and got on my nerves) and for making my career a lot easier to handle. Thanks for not agreeing with me all the time, since a true friend tells you when you're wrong. (I am right sometimes, though!) I appreciate your resilience and your vision, your patience and your understanding. (And I'm still not dealing with "Professional Arty"!)

To Kareem Moody of Moodswing Entertainment, thanks for being a promotional machine. You helped to make sure that people knew about my projects and that they supported my endeavors. I hope you know how much it has meant to me to have you in my corner. Thanks for motivating me and for being a true friend.

To the staff at Shaolin's finest beauty salon, *Lisa's Miracles,* thank you guys for always making me feel at home and for bigging me up every chance you get. Thank you for never being anything but friends to me. Ramiek, I could talk to you for hours. I love the light that comes from you and I love to see you smile. You are the bomb! Dee, you are so sweet and such a good person. Chanel, thanks for braiding me when I come in and for being Ashley's favorite stylist. Candy, thanks for making sure that whenever you're around, there is never a dull moment at Miracles. But most of all, thanks, Lisa. You are so much fun to be around. You would be my friend if you never did my hair again, because you are such a genuine person. Love ya. (And thank all of you for not being nearly as scandalous as the stylists at "Dime Piece"!)

To my fellow scribes who I've met on this literary journey. First and foremost, to Vickie Stringer T.C.P.'s (Triple Crown Publications) CEO/Publisher/Agent/Entrepreneur/Friend.
Thanks for allowing me to sit by your side and learn this industry. Thanks for your down to earth personality and for your advice and guidance. If you can wear as many hats as you do, and still stay on top, I know that I can write these books, raise these kids, juggle these responsibilities and still find time to spare. You lead by example and I admire you tremendously. I hope to work with you for years to come!

To Shannon Holmes, I want you to know that when you speak I am listening. Your words of wisdom and suggestions are not lost on me and I thank you for being a great example of success in this industry. I love your style and I wish you continued success.

To K'wan Foye and Nikki Turner, the two of you were the first to welcome me to the Triple Crown family, and I thank you for ushering me into this experience with your friendship. Both of you have great careers ahead of you, and I am humbled and honored to have my name listed on the same roster as the two of you. K'wan, you are so gifted and so prolific, that I am inspired by you. Nikki, you have a literary voice that is quite unique and your destiny is written. God bless you and your family.

Kashamba Williams, TN Baker, Trustice, JoyLynn Jossel, and all the other Triple Crown authors, let's continue to support and promote one another as we lock down this genre with teamwork. I am proud to work with all of you and consider myself blessed to work with such a committed, driven and talented group of writers. Continued success to each of you.

Mark Anthony, Al-Saadiq Banks, Asha Bandele, Carl Weber, and all the other authors I have connected with along the way, thanks for your encouragement and support.

To all the readers who come out to greet us at our book signings and tours, thanks for your love, your constructive criticism, your debates and your honesty. Without you, none of this would be worth doing. Thank you for reading our books and welcoming these characters into your imaginations. The greatest gift one can give to a writer is to read and understand their work and then to talk about it, to learn from it, to identify with it. Thanks so much to all the readers for your comments both positive and negative and thanks again for your love.

Introducing... Celeste Styles

Celeste threw the keys on the display case and flipped the light switch on in the salon. She flipped through the mail while she turned the radio on. "Bills, Bills, Bills" filled the speakers, and that's what Celeste saw as she sorted through the mail. Bills – all addressed to *Dime Piece* – her hair salon located in downtown Brooklyn. It was a Saturday morning in April 2000 and she knew the rain wouldn't keep anyone away. Easter was the next day, and Celeste knew from experience that the shop would be busy. She told the stylists to arrive early and be ready to get money.

But no one was there yet. It was 8 am, and she didn't expect any of the girls to arrive for about an hour. Celeste liked to be a step ahead of the pack and get her paper straight before the day began. So she often arrived early, never expecting that someone might be watching that. But as she walked toward the back of the shop, where the dryers were located behind an Asian patterned partition, she noticed something wasn't right. She saw that the back door seemed slightly ajar and instinctively she drew her gun. But before she could raise it, someone rushed her from behind and grabbed her arm. Under his grip, she dropped the gun. He covered her mouth and dragged and carried her small 5'5" frame toward her office in the back. She sensed right away that he knew her safe was in there and she fought him with all her might.

To her surprise, he pushed her against her cherry wood desk and she hit her head. As she recovered, dazed, he gun butted her dead in the face. She realized that without her gun she couldn't fight this dude. He meant business. He straddled her and pulled her hair until her face was inches from his. She could smell alcohol on his breath and feel his desperation as she looked in his eyes, though she was still in a daze. He wore a black ski mask, so all she could see were his cold, hungry eyes.

"Open the fuckin safe." He said it calmly in a deep, raspy voice and cocked his gun. "Now."

Celeste knew she couldn't win, so she slowly inched toward the safe. With his gun at her temple, she entered the combination and unlocked the fortress that held close to $100,000 of Rah-Lo's money as well as her own. She wished she could somehow summon Rah-Lo at that moment while the intruder pillaged her hard earned cash and held her at bay with the barrel of his Glock 9. Rah-Lo was her man, one of the most revered hustlers in town, and a nigga whose name was respected like few others in the game. Rah-Lo was nothing to fuck with and everyone admired him. He was a generous man who sponsored the local basketball team and gave food baskets to the impoverished families in the hood during the holidays. Though he was married to another woman who had birthed his two daughters, Celeste had long been the chick on the side. She likened her situation to Lil Kim's position in the life of the Notorious B.I.G. While B.I.G was married to Faith Evans, and it was she who held the title of "Mrs. Wallace", Lil Kim had always been a force to be reckoned with. Where there was B.I.G., there was Kim; sort of a hood Bonnie and Clyde story. And just like Kim, Celeste played her position. She was very well kept. Rah-Lo kept her securely tucked away in a mini mansion he owned in Staten Island. Her lifestyle was the envy of all women.

Most important, though, was the significance of the
chance this intruder was taking by robbing Celeste. Rah-Lo
would surely kill this man if he ever found out his identity.
But this masked muthafucka obviously didn't give a damn.
He took all the dough and secured it in a blue duffle bag he
brought. He placed it by the door; never taking his eyes off
of Celeste for fear that she might have a gun in her office.
She cowered in the corner by the safe, still wearing her safari
green hooded jacket and watched in horror as he advanced
towards her.

Why wasn't he leaving? He had the money. Celeste
began to panic as the stranger scooped her up roughly and
laid her across the top of the desk, knocking over everything,
from her phone to the pictures of Rah-Lo. His back was
facing the open door and he tugged at her jeans. She
struggled mightily and kicked at his groin. But he
overpowered her; he manhandled her as she writhed against
him. He ripped open her shirt and tore off her bra as she
fought him off. He slapped her brutally and she tried to
resist him as he pulled her jeans down to her ankles despite
her scratching and biting, clawing at him. He pushed her
panties aside with one hand and held her face still with his
palm over her mouth and his fingers splayed across her nose
and eyes. She continued to fight but it only seemed to make
him more determined. Her exposed breasts jiggled as he
fought to enter her and she felt so violated. She started to
cry in frustration and he laughed at her fighting so hard. He
said, "Yeah, bitch. Go 'head and cry!"

With her free hand she punched at him as best she
could in the awkward position she was in. He didn't let up.
She continued to cry and to scream but her torment didn't
bother this man. He laughed at her, breathing heavily in her
face. But as the stranger's dick stood ready to invade her,
Celeste saw a gun aimed straight at his temple. It seemed
like slow motion from that point on. When the shot was

fired, spraying the nigga's brain matter all over the office windows, Celeste screamed and shuddered, terrified. The shot had been fired so close to her that she heard ringing in her ears. She felt dizzy. She wriggled out from under the stranger's dead body and looked in the direction of the shooter who had saved her from a vicious rape. She was not concerned about her exposed upper body. Celeste was furious, traumatized and hysterical. Her vision blurred by tears, she soon realized that the gunman was none other than Ishmael – Rah-Lo's partner and right hand man. She cried and pulled her jacket closed around her, embarrassed by her vulnerability. But Ishmael walked to her and held his arms open. He placed the gun – her gun that she had dropped on the floor when she entered – on the shelf and walked slowly in her direction.

　　"Relax, Ma. That nigga's dead. You alright?" Her clothes were disheveled and she tried to cover herself. Ishmael diverted his gaze and noticed Celeste's trembling body. "It's alright, baby girl. I'm gonna call Rah-Lo…"

　　Celeste was distraught. "Thank God you came when you did…" Her voice trailed off as she cried.

　　While Celeste fixed her tattered clothing, Ishmael explained how fate had landed him at her shop so early in the morning. "I just left my man's crib and shit. I was on my way to get some breakfast and on my way down the block, I saw your car." Ishmael calmly wiped the prints off the gun. "I stopped to find out if you wanted somethin'' to eat and I found this shit goin' on." Ishmael shook his head. "I saw your gun on the floor out front and I picked that shit up and came in here." Both Ishmael and Celeste wondered who the stranger was, so Ishmael pulled the mask back to reveal the dead man's face. Both of them reacted from the recognition.

　　"Dre!" Celeste was immediately angry. "That muthafucka was supposed to be Rah-Lo's friend." Ishmael shook his head knowing that in the game, there's no such thing as "friends". But even he was surprised that the nigga

Dre would have the nerve to target Rah-Lo's money *and* his woman.

"I'ma call Rah-Lo and tell him what happened. We gotta clean this up, you know what I'm sayin'?" Ishmael put the gun beside Dre's corpse. "You're gonna need a new gun." Celeste pulled herself together as best she could. Despite his calming voice, Celeste knew Ishmael well enough to sense his rage. The veins in his forearms bulged as he paced the room dialing Rah-Lo's number while Celeste ran to lock the shop door. She grabbed the duffel bag full of money and emptied the contents back into the safe, locking it securely. Then she sat trembling in the corner with her head in her hands, trying to block out what happened to her and waiting for Rah-Lo to come and make it alright.

"Don't worry, Celeste," Ishmael said. "I'm here now. I got you. Ain't nobody gonna hurt you as long as I'm here."

His words were reassuring and Celeste took deep breaths to calm herself. She looked over at Ishmael. He was taking off his blood-spattered shirt and his body was well toned underneath. She thanked God for Ishmael. The two of them had always been close. But who knew he would one day save her from the unthinkable? She felt a gratitude wash over her that sent chills up her spine. She let herself cry and Ishmael comforted her. She began to feel relief after allowing herself to cry and Ishmael continued to hold and console her. Celeste couldn't help wondering if she had ever felt as safe in another man's arms as she did at that moment in Ishmael's.

Raheem "Rah-Lo" Henderson to the Rescue

After about twenty-five minutes, Rah-Lo and four of his boys arrived. While Ishmael and the rest went about their business removing the body and tampering with evidence, Rah-Lo held and comforted Celeste, telling her that he loved her and that he would die if another man had her. He cradled her close to him and was obviously sincere judging from the tears in his eyes. "I owe Ishmael for saving you from that muthafucka." Rah-Lo said. Using the back door, which led to a nearly deserted residential block behind the Brooklyn beauty shop, Ishmael and the rest of the guys took Dre's body out to a waiting car. As the time neared for the arrival of customers and stylists, one of the guys brought in a big garbage bag and entered Celeste's office, closing the door behind him. Rah-Lo held Celeste's hand and explained what was happening. "He's gonna clean the scene up, make sure we got everything. Act like nothin' happened and tell your customers that the shop ain't opening until 10:00. Let your workers know that they gotta stay from back here while we handle our business."

So Celeste fought to control her frazzled nerves as she took her seat at the front of the shop. She felt like Rah-Lo wanted her to just pull herself together, but Celeste was traumatized. She knew that it went along with the territory since she was fuckin' with a hustler. Rah-Lo was the nigga to see. He had a reputation that was legacy throughout the boroughs. He also had some enemies that prayed for his downfall. Dre was evidence of that. At one point, Dre had been one of Rah-Lo's young apprentices. But obviously somewhere along the line, shit got twisted. Something had apparently transpired between Rah-Lo and Dre. And poor Celeste was caught in the middle. She was a casualty of war. Rah-Lo knew that no one would ever be able to touch a hair on his wife's head. Asia was the mother of his children, so he always ensured that they were safe and secure in his home and under his lieutenants' constant watch. But he felt terrible about Celeste being victimized. Knowing that he couldn't always be around to protect her, Rah-Lo had given her the gun for protection in case anything ever happened while they were apart. He never thought that she would still be in danger.

Strangely, despite her love for Rah-Lo, Celeste felt angry with him for being the reason she was targeted in the first place. Before she started dealing with Rah-Lo, nothing like this would have ever happened to her. She was mad that his lifestyle had put her in such a vulnerable position. At the same time that she was feeling some contempt for Rah-Lo, she was feeling enormous gratitude for Ishmael. But she pushed those feelings to the back of her mind; brushed them off as a reaction to her ordeal. Ishmael had been the one to save her, after all. And Rah-Lo had been nowhere in sight.

A customer or two arrived and Celeste calmly explained that a flood by the sinks was making it necessary to delay the shop's opening by an hour. Once they were gone, the stylists began to arrive. Celeste noticed that Nina arrived first. Nina greeted Celeste and she busied herself setting up her station, plugging in hot irons and laying out her combs and scissors. Celeste appreciated the fact that Nina came ready to get her hustle on. It was all about the

Benjamins and as long as Nina kept bringing in the dough, she was alright with Celeste. Nina was a pretty girl, brown skinned with stunning features, a perfect bone structure and a head full of long, lustrous hair. Nina came from a very difficult background. The way Celeste saw it, Nina was constantly seeking the attention and affection that had eluded her for a lifetime. Her personality had a tendency to turn people off – particularly women. But she was cool people and a hard worker. Nina was the ideal employee. That was all that mattered to Celeste.

Soon after, Charly strolled in wearing a Baby Phat sweat suit. The jiggle that she had when she walked in and headed for her station, showed that she obviously wore no panties. Charly was sexy and she knew it. She stood 5'7" with an hourglass figure and an expensive weave. Her high yellow skin tone and light eyes made her appear almost exotic. But let her open her mouth and you'd immediately know that she was from around the way. Charly was hood, through and through. But she had men wrapped around her finger and she seemed to do it effortlessly. She was a jet setter, due in part to the fact that she seemed to always attract ballers and soon to be moguls. Charly used all of her assets to her full advantage. She began to set up her workstation, too, watching as Celeste turned away several more customers. She wondered why the shop was opening late, but she didn't question Celeste. Charly took in the scene, tying her black smock around her slim waist.

Last to arrive was Robin. She was the calm one. She was a nice, young girl – only nineteen and on her own. She was also the single mother of a one-year-old son Hezekiah, so Celeste allowed her more leniencies in terms of punctuality. But sometimes she had to remind her that being on time was not a suggestion but a requirement. Robin was short, a pint sized, size two spitfire with a good head on her shoulders despite her bad decisions. Robin had a flawless reputation with her clientele, which consisted of mostly men and young children. She was the braider, the one who had the job of making sure the little girls would look pretty in church the next day and that the guys had their locks freshly twisted for the occasion.

All the girls had arrived by 9:25 and Celeste called them all together for a meeting. "This morning the shop was robbed and that's why we have to open late."

Each lady gasped or stood stunned as Celeste explained that the intruder had gotten away and Rah-Lo and his crew were securing the premises for the rest of the day. The sound of a vacuum being used in Celeste's office caused Robin to look over her shoulder in that direction.

"I don't wanna close the shop today because there's so much money to be made. This is one of our busiest weekends of the year!"

Charly agreed. "Word. If them niggas was smart, they woulda waited to hit this place until today's money came in." Charly was straight hood. "I don't know about everybody else, but I need this money today. I'm working."

Nina and Robin agreed. Celeste instructed the stylists not to mention the robbery to the clients and warned them about their own money. She managed to conveniently leave out the details of her own close call. Celeste kept the details of the dreadful experience to herself. "Niggas might be watching us, noticing how we're coming and going, so be careful. Please watch your backs. We're all like family up in here and I don't wanna see none of us hurt by some broke ass busta."

Charly noticed that Celeste was shaking – trembling ever so slightly. She saw that Rah-Lo was very comforting towards Celeste after the quick meeting ended, and she couldn't help but wonder what exactly had happened in the shop that morning. She noticed Ishmael come in from the back and he talked in hushed tones with Rah-Lo. Before he left, Ishmael went over and hugged Celeste a little longer than what was usual. Charly took it all in. She exchanged glances with Ishmael's fine ass as he passed her on his way out the back door. After about ten more minutes passed, all but one of Rah-Lo's boys had left and the atmosphere was tense and quiet. But within a half an hour, the shop opened and the customers poured in. All the stylists were quickly so busy that their minds drifted away from the events of the morning. The radio, programmed to Hot 97, was a pleasant diversion as Biggie's gruff voice boomed from the overhead speakers.

Rah-Lo urged Celeste to go home and recuperate from the trauma of what almost happened to her. She eventually gave in, leaving Nina in charge while she went home to take a nap. Rah-Lo escorted her to his car – a black Lincoln Navigator – parked at the corner. Rah-Lo drove towards the Verrazano Bridge; headed for Staten Island. Celeste lived in a sizable estate Rah-Lo owned on Howard Avenue. It was an exclusive community of sprawling homes and wealthy homeowners. It was also one piece of property that he owned that his wife knew nothing about. In addition to the Staten Island home, there was a Queens townhouse he kept without his wife's knowledge. Asia never questioned him. He kept her happy with the comforts his wealth afforded her. She kept to herself and didn't keep many women around her. Thus, she never heard about Celeste during the time she had spent as Rah-Lo's wifey. And Celeste, being secure in her position, never bragged about her exploits with Rah-Lo. She was discreet, happy and content with the extent of her relationship with Rah-Lo.

Rah-Lo had always taken care of Celeste – in fact he had been that way with all his women. If a chick was with Rah-Lo, he always made sure she had the hottest car, the flyest clothes, and her hair was always done. But Celeste had something that caused her to stand out from the rest. She had a good head on her shoulders. Yes, she drove the car that Rah-Lo bought her – a black 2000 Pathfinder – and lived in the home he provided for her. But Celeste wanted ownership. She wanted a business that she could call her own. Something that would remain long after the car and the house were gone. Rah-Lo admired the fact that Celeste had dreams, which she wasn't afraid to chase. Most of the women he came in contact with were only concerned with being beautiful. They wanted a sponsor; someone to finance their shopping sprees and keep them laced. So he bankrolled *Dime Piece* as a gift to her. That was a big step for Rah-Lo. Up to that point, he had never put a thing in a woman's name. Rah-Lo had loved other women and enjoyed the intimate company of more than his share, but in his eyes, there was something sweet about Celeste. He loved her and he had a weakness in his heart when it came to her. In fact, he would kill a nigga over Celeste. But still someone had dared to try and violate her body.

And his boy Ishmael had come to her rescue. Rah-Lo felt grateful to Ishmael for saving her. Rah-Lo would have blown the muthafuckas brains out himself had he had the chance. He looked over at his beautiful wifey as she stared silently out the passenger side window. She was an exquisite woman, sepia colored with a smile that would melt the coldest heart. Her makeup was always flawless. Long thick lashes accentuated her gorgeous eyes and they lit up when she smiled. Her appearance was always stunning.

Rah-Lo couldn't help but note the difference in the woman by his side and the wife he had at home. Asia was rowdy; hood through and through. Theirs was a passionate relationship, both in the bedroom and in the arguments they had almost daily. Celeste, on the other hand, was classy and refined, having been raised with grace by a doting single mother and her loving, church-going Christian grandmother. They stressed education; Celeste *had* to go to college. They wanted a future for her as a Black woman independently wealthy. Those women raised her with femininity, class and grace. She was a gem. But Celeste had been raised in the hood and the girls she rolled with didn't have parents with lofty expectations of them. She always envied them because they were able to choose their own paths in life – go to trade school or try to break into the music industry – while Celeste was only allowed to choose which college she would go to. She was drawn to the magnetism of street life. In high school, she would say she was studying with classmates and then sneak off to the club. As soon as she was old enough, she got herself a one-bedroom apartment with the money her mother gave her for graduation. She started out with $5,000 and a plan. Celeste was hustling her way towards a bachelor's degree as a Business major and doing hair on the side to keep the lights on. But she was free. For the first time, she had a private life. She liked men with an edge more than the ones with from her Anthropology class. Thus, she fell in love with a thug - Rah-Lo. He was the love of her life. Rah-Lo was the sexiest man she'd ever known.

A Chance Encounter

They met in 1992 when she and a couple of friends went for a "waiting to exhale" style drive through the slums of Shaolin. Celeste was attending Medgar Evers College in Brooklyn and she was close with two fellow students. Erin was from Staten Island (Shaolin) and April was from uptown in Harlem. It was a summer night, and they decided to try Erin's borough out for a change. Staten Island was the "other borough". Not your usual hot spot. But that particular evening, they gave it a shot. Erin was driving with Celeste riding shotgun and April in the backseat. Erin was an aspiring physical therapist and April was working for transit while pursuing a Communications degree part time. The ladies were all in their early twenties, nursing broken hearts and still looking for love.

Discussing their love lives and the drama involved in the same, they relaxed and unwound listening to Mary's "What's the 411" while passing a haze filled blunt between them. Starting out in the Harbor, where Erin was from, they drove through West Brighton, New Brighton, Stapleton and finally Park Hill. It was a warm summer night, and as they drove along Park Hill Avenue, they noticed the abundance of people sprinkled up and down the block. Car radios blared, people laughed and yelled to one another from open windows. Park Hill had an energy that was unmatched in the borough.

"Now, I *like* it out here," April said, with her head out the window checking out the thuggish beefcake up and down the block.

When they drove past 55 Bowen and turned right on Targee Street, Erin pulled the car over because she saw Pappy. He was a guy Erin was falling hard for – a shady nigga with shady dealings and a shady past.

"I'll be right back, y'all. Let me holla at my baby real quick." Erin slid out the car before her friends could protest.

As he stood posted up on the block, Erin sashayed sexily in his direction. Pappy seemed surprised to see her and they talked with their faces inches apart.

Looking at the dashboard clock, Celeste noted that it was well past 10pm and she was supposed to do her friend Bridget's hair. She decided to hop out of the car and call her at the payphone across the street at the gas station. She told April where she was going and stepped out of the car into the balmy August evening. The arcade, which they were parked in front of, was packed with niggas and when Celeste stepped out the car wearing skintight jeans and a fitted black tank top and black sandals, the arcade emptied out. At least ten guys poured onto the sidewalk calling out to the sexy shorty none of them had seen before.

"Come here, ma. Let me holla at you."

"Damn, baby. You *wearin'* them jeans!"

"Sweet thing. Can I talk to you?"

Celeste was flattered but she kept right on stepping. She didn't respond well to catcalls. It would take more than a snappy line or a nice compliment to get Celeste's attention. She walked over to the payphone and picked up the receiver, she was just about to dial when one of the guys crossed the street in her direction with a walk that was sexy as hell.

"Excuse me. Can I talk to you for a minute?" He asked, flashing her a devilish grin as he approached.

"I apologize for my friends. It ain't everyday that they see somebody as fly as you are steppin' out on the block. My name is Rah-Lo." He extended his hand and Celeste hesitated before she shook it. Upon seeing her shake his outstretched hand, the other block huggers gave up any hope of baggin' her and began retreating back inside the arcade while the rest of Park Hill milled around outside. "Don't talk to *him*, ma, I'm the one you want," one of the men yelled across the street. Rah-Lo ignored the remark and continued to gaze at the sexy lady before him. Looking over Rah-Lo's shoulder, Celeste saw that Erin was still occupied with Pappy.

"You ain't gonna tell me your name?" Rah-Lo asked, still grinning. He leaned against the phone booth, blocking her view to ensure that he had her undivided attention.

"My name is Celeste." She said it with a smile and that was all the encouragement Rah-Lo needed. He dove right in.

"You look good, Celeste. A nigga would have to be blind not to notice that, you know what I'm sayin'? And I ain't tryin' to run no game on you or no shit like that. I just wanted to tell you that you like *nice*." He looked her dead in the eye the entire time and his eyes looked so sincere.

Immediately, Celeste knew it was all game. She could tell that this wasn't the first time this guy had stepped to a female since he did it so effortlessly. But she still admired his style. He had a confidence she hadn't seen in a man so young. And to Celeste, nothing was sexier than a man with confidence. The fact that he was the only one with enough guts to cross the street and risk rejection scored high points with her.

"Thank you very much." They looked in each other's eyes during the lull in conversation. Rah-Lo was thinking about how good she must look outside of those jeans. Celeste was wondering what kind of game he was playing. Then Erin called from across the street.

Then Erin called to her from across the street, "Come on, Celeste!" Erin yelled, climbing back behind the wheel as Pappy strolled up the block.

Rah-Lo looked over his shoulder in Erin's direction then turned back to Celeste. "Let me get your number before you go."

She shook her head. "I ain't giving you my number. I don't even know you."

"You know something? I don't know you either. So let me get your number and we can get to know each other."

"If I see you again, I'll give it to you then." Celeste started to walk away but Rah-Lo tugged gently at her hand.

"What if I never see you again? I don't wanna take that chance. Where you from?"

"I'm from Brooklyn."

"See? I'm scared of Brooklyn." Rah-Lo said it, smiling. Celeste laughed at his wit. "What if we never cross paths again?"

Celeste laughed. "You don't strike me as the type to be scared of anything."

Rah-Lo grinned again. "I'm scared you're gonna walk off without giving me your number."

Erin beeped the horn impatiently. Celeste hesitated. She looked at Rah-Lo. He was cute. He stood about 6'0" and he had a nice build; almond colored sex appeal wrapped in a tough package. She liked his thugged out demeanor and his round the way swagger. He was cocky yet disarming. He was a smooth talker and he intrigued her. She had no idea why, but she liked this guy.

"917-0001."

She said it and strolled back to her friends waiting in the car. Before she climbed into the passenger seat, she looked back at Rah-Lo, expecting him to be writing down her number. Instead, she saw him leaning against the phone booth, waving goodbye. It was the start of an unparalleled love.

He called her two days later. They talked for a while, and learned a little about each other. She said, "I thought you lost my number."

Rah-Lo answered, "I couldn't lose it. I never wrote it down to begin with. I just remembered it."

Celeste was skeptical. "Whatever."

"Nah, that's my word. I never write stuff down. People get in trouble like that." She could tell right away what his lifestyle was. She knew a dozen thugs jus like him; many of them were among her countless cousins and uncles. Celeste was no stranger to seedy characters. But she liked his style, admired his intellect and he was disarming. They met up at the movies and saw Spike Lee's "X". The movie sparked an interesting debate between Celeste and Rah-Lo about the Nation of Islam and its role in Malcolm's death. She found herself surprised at how broad Rah-Lo's knowledge was. He was from the gutter, a hustler with a PHD from the school of hard knocks. And yet he had a conversation with her about the civil rights movement that impressed her. He knew so much about so many things. She found herself impressed by his ability to disagree without being disagreeable. She found herself letting down her guard.

They wound up back at her small apartment on Bedford Avenue, watching Showtime at the Apollo. Jodeci was performing that night, and they sat on Celeste's sofa watching the show. Rah-Lo put his arm around Celeste and she didn't mind. K-Ci sang his heart out and Rah-Lo kissed Celeste softly.   DeVante had the ladies in the audience swooning as Rah-Lo held Celeste closer. JoJo sang on his knees and Rah-Lo had his hands on Celeste's breasts. When the camera cut to Mr. Dalvin, Celeste wanted to fuck Rah-Lo so badly. She had to force herself to say, "Nah, I can't do this…"

"Please, Celeste." Rah-Lo's eyes pleaded. "I want you." He seemed hungry for her.

"But…" He muzzled her with his kisses. She tried to tell herself she'd regret it. "I don't want you to think…"

"I won't think shit. I swear. I swear I won't look at you different."

He seemed sincere. And he felt so good. She couldn't resist it anymore. She gave in, and they devoured each other, both of them consumed with infatuation and passion. She was in ecstasy when he slid a condom on and penetrated her. She thought fleetingly about how he conveniently had a condom in his pocket and she surmised that he probably knew he could get the panties on the first night. So she fucked him wildly. She put her all into it and matched his intensity. She figured this was probably a game to him and she would never hear from him again. So she gave it her all for the first and last time. She wanted to be sure that he wouldn't forget the sex! It wasn't long before Rah-Lo couldn't help but bust and he lay on top of her sweaty and breathless.

They looked in each other's eyes. And Rah-Lo kissed her gently on the lips, then went to her bathroom and got a towel. He came back and cleaned her off first and then himself. That shit scored *major* points with Celeste. It was usually the woman cleaning the *man* off, not the other way around. Rah-Lo had her wondering if chivalry was really dead.

He stayed the night, sleeping in his boxer shorts with his head laying in her lap as she reclined on the couch. At about 5am, he woke her and explained that he had to get back on the grind. She thought she'd never see him again as she walked him out and watched him drive away.

But Rah-Lo called the next day. And the day after that. And before long, they were official like Bonnie and Clyde. Mickey and Mallory. He wasn't turned off by the fact that she gave it up to him so soon. They were both grown and they knew they wanted each other. Celeste was unlike any other woman he had dealt with. She stimulated his mind as well as his body and she gave him encouragement and constructive criticism. He schooled her on the way of the streets and taught her the art of survival. And in return, she gave him stimulating conversation and wonderful sex and he loved her. Plus she was always fly. Her hair was always flawless, and she wore very little makeup. She was a sight for sore eyes. Rah-Lo admired that she was going to school and getting her hustle on by doing hair. She was good at what she did, too. She had a nice little clientele just working out of her customer's kitchens. No matter how much dough Rah-Lo spent on her, Celeste always had her own. He loved that about her.

As months passed, they spent all the time together they could. She let him keep his drugs at her house. He gave her the combination to his safe. She strapped packages to her body and boarded trains out of state for him. He made her his priority and they fell in love like they never dreamed possible. Rah-Lo didn't admit to Celeste he was married until she found out the hard way. They were at a party together at the Island Room, a nightclub in Staten Island. Celeste had gone to use the ladies room, and upon returning found Rah-Lo talking to a woman who had her arms draped intimately around his neck. Celeste headed over, ready for a confrontation. But as she approached, Rah-Lo intercepted her. "Hi, Celeste. I haven't seen you in a while. This is my wife, Asia," he said. He was playing it off, trying to act like Celeste was an old acquaintance he hadn't seen for a long time. Asia had no idea that she was face to face with Rah-Lo's mistress.

Celeste stood dumbfounded wondering if she had heard Rah-Lo correctly. As Asia looked in her direction, scowling, Celeste noted the big diamond band on her slender light-skinned finger. Asia was a pretty woman, but Celeste couldn't believe she was Rah-Lo's wife. She turned and walked away without responding.

Rah-Lo came by her apartment that night, and had his first argument with Celeste. She was devastated, and Rah-Lo apologized for hiding the truth. He told Celeste that he didn't love his wife like he loved her. Their marriage was one of convenience. If it wasn't for his daughters, he would have left long ago. But he respected Asia enough to keep his dirt so far from home that the two worlds never collided. Celeste was his heart and he vowed that as long as she continued to ride for him, he would keep her happy for as long as he could. Despite the voice in her head telling her not to settle for a man she had to share – not to settle for second best – Celeste loved Rah-Lo, and she yielded.

Years passed, and Rah-Lo built his dream team. Things started looking up and they all handled business. Celeste started spending more and more time in Shaolin and eventually, she moved into his house on Howard Avenue to be closer to him. She fell in love with life in his world. She adapted quickly and began to make him a happy home. But Brooklyn was always her first love and she spent a lot of time there with her family and friends. She enjoyed the tranquility Staten Island offered her and the convenience of being Brooklyn's close neighbor.

One day in 1993 on Bay Street, Celeste was shopping for hair products in a beauty supply store when she met Charly. Charly was working for some African men who owned a salon and she asked Celeste where she got her hair done. When Celeste told her that she did it herself, Charly was impressed. Celeste complimented Charly on her own lovely hair and was surprised when Charly told her it was a full weave. The two became instant friends. That bond proved mutually beneficial when Rah-Lo blessed Celeste with her own business. Celeste brought Charly on board as her star stylist. Rah-Lo watched his sweetheart parlay her friendship into a lucrative business and he was so proud of her. After years in the business, Celeste hired more stylists. Now, she only worked by appointment – on her own terms – and she knew in her heart that her mother was proud, although she never said it. Celeste had made it, and no one could take that away from her.

The Chickens Come Home to Roost

As Celeste laid her head against the passenger door she closed her eyes to stop the image of her attacker in the black ski mask. She tried to block out the memory of how it felt to have the bastard's hands on her – how it felt to be defenseless against him. Rah-Lo looked over at her and stroked her cheek. "I won't ever let nobody hurt you, baby girl. I'm sorry."

She knew he felt guilty about what happened. Rah-Lo had been Dre's real target. Celeste was just a link in the chain. And she was beginning to wonder if being in love with Rah-Lo was worth the dangerous situations she found herself in. Her stoic and resilient demeanor was gone and now she was a shell of her former self. Celeste was upset and understandably so.

Rah-Lo explained the situation. "I found out the nigga Dre owed his soul to the devil. Everybody and they mama was after him for owing them money. I guess he was desperate or some shit. He needed the money, but rather than ask me like a man, he did some dumb shit. But for him to try to take you like that…" Rah-Lo shook his head, the thought leaving him beyond words.

When they got to the house, Rah-Lo electronically opened the door of the two-car garage and parked his truck. They entered the house through the downstairs door and headed upstairs to his bedroom. Celeste lay across the bed. She was longing for sleep – a way to escape from the constant replay of the day in her mind. She lay in a fetal position and tucked her hands under her cheek. She closed her eyes and tried to think of something other than the day's events. Rah-Lo stood in the doorway staring at her, wishing there was something he could do to make her feel better. He shook his head in frustration and left the room, and headed downstairs for the kitchen. The kitchen was large with a smoky, charcoal gray finish. The splashes of white and subtle color throughout the room came from plants and flower arrangements Celeste was the one to thank for those housewarming touches. Rah-Lo pulled a beer from the fridge and cracked the top. He guzzled it until he nearly choked, coughing slightly and then walked into the living room.

Rah-Lo realized that things were getting out of control. Dre was one of the young'ns that he was trying to bring up in the game. There were lots of young men like that in the hood. They wanted what they saw Rah-Lo and his cohorts enjoying. They wanted the wealth and the women, the riches and the recognition. All of that came with a price, though. There were situations that Rah-Lo found himself in during his lifetime that he wished he had never been through. Every man has a conscience, and Rah-Lo was no exception. He had earned his stripes and he had his own demons to battle because of it. Rah-Lo still had respect for the young lost boys coming up in the streets. He remembered having that same hunger and the yearning for better days. He admired a youngster with a dream and the drive to achieve it. But that sonofabitch Dre decided to cut corners and take what didn't belong to him. And Rah-Lo was mad at himself; frustrated that he hadn't seen the signs. He hadn't noticed the fact that one of his underlings was scheming on his empire right under his own nose. Rah-Lo wondered if he was slipping, if he was falling off. Muthafuckas wanted his spot. Niggas was coming for his head and he had to be on point at all times.

It was time to take inventory; time to give out some hollow point pink slips; it was necessary that Rah-Lo get his business under control. There was a need for change and Rah-Lo made a decision to weed out the good and bad in his cipher.

Back at the shop in Brooklyn, Ishmael came back to check on the safety of the premises. He had a couple of his dogs in tow in case he needed them. Ishmael sat on Nina's stool while she applied a relaxer to a client's new growth. He spoke briefly with Nina about locking up the shop since Celeste was at home resting. Ishmael was also glancing at Nina's sexy figure as she stood inches from him.

"What if I'm scared to lock up?" she asked, sexily blinking her eyes, which were false and full. Ishmael liked her body but he didn't know her well.

"I could make sure you get home alright" He said it rather suggestively. "Just hit me on my cell when you're ready to bounce."

He gossiped with her about a fight that broke out earlier that day in the barbershop across the street. Then Ishmael prepared to leave. But as he passed Charly, who was washing a pretty young girl's hair at the sink, she called out to him.

"Wassup, Ish?" He took notice of her flattering attire and the way her booty bounced in her pants as she scrubbed the girl's hair.

"Wassup withchu, beautiful?" he asked. "I haven't seen you in a while." Ishmael had always noticed Charly with the trendy clothes and brick house physique. But she always seemed too busy to speak. Until that day.

"I'm chillin'",she said. "Just trying to get this money, you know?" She turned on the hose and rinsed the lady's hair as she spoke.

Ishmael stopped walking and checked Charly out from head to toe. Liking what he saw, he said, "You workin' till Nina locks up tonight?"

He was thrilled when Charly nodded that she would be there. "I'll take you home, if you need a ride," Ishmael said it offhandedly.

"Thanks." Charly licked her lips subtly. "I'll see you later on, then."

Ishmael left with his boys in tow. Robin watched the way both Charly and Nina went weak-kneed over Ishmael and she shook her head. She had no time to pursue any man, but Ishmael *was* fine. He was tall with a warm cocoa complexion. He had a slim goatee that was always crisp. His style was exquisite and he was always the flamboyant type. When Ishmael stepped on the scene, everyone looked to see what clothes he was wearing, which jewels he was wearing, and which broad had his attention. Even those who disliked him had to admit that his flair for the spotlight was unmatched. Though he was calm and quiet on the surface, those who knew him also knew there lurked a dark side of Ishmael's character.

But to Robin none of that mystery and stylishness was impressive. She had a son to raise and a future to secure. She set about her business, washing her customer's hair, while Charly quietly counted down the hours until Ishmael's return.

Charly Hanson

Charly was unplugging her hot plate and putting some stray strands of weave into her storage bin. The last customer had finally left, and she was ready to go home and take a shower. She was still trying to decide which plans she would follow through with that Saturday night. Charly had cancelled her ride home with a guy she was thinking about going out with, opting instead to tag along with Ishmael. She wasn't thrilled about the fact that Nina would also be getting a ride home with him. Charly wanted Ishmael all to herself. But as she looked at her Fendi watch with the diamonds in the bezel, she realized that it was already 10pm, and Ishmael was nowhere in sight. *'This nigga better hurry up and get here. Shit, Charly Hanson is NOT to be kept waiting',* she thought to herself.

Nina sat in her chair, watching Charly pace the shop busying herself with minor things like sweeping the floor, which Robin had already swept moments earlier. *'Look at her fiending for Ishmael to get here. She's like a vulture, circling its prey. Damn!'* But, beknownst only to herself, Nina was also anxious to see Ishmael again. She smiled to herself, knowing that since her house in Fort Green was closer to Ishmael's house in Clinton Hill, she would most likely be dropped off last, giving her valuable alone time with him. Charly lived all the way in Staten Island, which was about a twenty-five-minute drive from the shop. Nina's smile broadened as she imagined herself in the front seat of Ishmael's car, taking the long way home.

Robin, however, was concerned only about her son. She had to pick him up from her sister's house before her sister had a fit. Robin's sister, Sunday, was younger than her. She lived at home with her parents, and she was a college freshman. Sunday had done all the things that Robin hadn't done herself. Robin's decision to drop out of college during her freshman year was something she was learning to live with. Robin had fallen in love. Her son's father was a guy named Juno, a small time hustler from Queens. Despite the fact that Juno wasn't seeing Robin exclusively, he was supportive of her pregnancy. Hezekiah would have been the first child for both of them. But, six weeks before Robin was due to give birth, Juno was killed on the same block he did his dirt on. Robin had been on her own ever since, struggling to get by and determined not to have to eat crow and go back home to her parents' house. She would make it on her own, come hell or high water, and she would make sure that Hezekiah never wanted for nothing.

But since Sunday had the ideal life, she was anxious to get out of the house and get into the club. She was calling Robin every five minutes, begging her to come and pick up her son. Robin hated to think that Hezekiah was a burden to anybody and she cursed under her breath, frustrated that the babysitter had canceled on her at the last minute, forcing her to ask for her sister's help. Robin grabbed her car keys off her workstation, looked at Nina and Charly nearly bursting in anticipation of seeing Ishmael again and she shook her head, disgusted. *'If these two only knew that nigga's ain't shit but heartache and pain rolled up in a sexy package.'* Robin said goodnight to the both of them and headed out to her black Honda Civic parked outside.

Now, Charly and Nina were alone, and the silence was awkward. Nina tried to fill it. "So what you getting into tonight, Charly? You going to church in the morning?" Nina was being sarcastic and Charly knew it.

"Nah. I wont be in church, Nina. Hopefully, I'll be sittin' up in some nigga's house with him feeding me breakfast in bed."

Nina grinned at Charly. "Which nigga will it be this time?" Nina knew her verbal dart had hit the bullseye when Charly's smile turned into a frown.

Just as Charly was about to let Nina have it, the shop door swung open and Ishmael came strolling in. Charly looked at Nina. "Maybe this one will do," she said, causing Nina to scowl at Charly as if to say, 'Over my dead body!'

"Wassup, ladies? Y'all ready to go?"

Charly and Nina told him they were very ready to go, and they turned off all the lights and prepared to leave. Since Nina had the keys to the shop, when they stepped out into the cool April evening, she began to secure the shop's doors. By the time she turned to walk to the car, she realized that Charly had positioned herself in the passenger seat, where she was giggling and flirting with sexy ass Ishmael. Nina was pissed! Resigning herself to the back seat, she climbed inside and got comfortable in Ishmael's Suburban. Charly was hogging his attention, telling him about how her car was stolen weeks earlier. Charly had a Maxima and she adored that car almost as much as she adored herself. But she came out of the Staten Island mall, fresh off one of her male-financed shopping sprees, and her car had been stolen. Ishmael listened sympathetically as Nina squirmed in the backseat. It wasn't long before she realized that they were only a block away from Nina's own apartment in Fort Greene.

"Ishmael, you should drop Charly off in Shaolin first since you live so close to where I live. I don't mind taking that ride with you." Nina smiled to hide her frustration.

Ishmael smiled back, looking at Nina through the rearview mirror. "I was gonna do that, ma. But Charly asked if I could help her change a light bulb in her apartment, so I'll take you home first."

Charly turned around to face Nina in the backseat. "You know how I have those *high* cathedral ceilings in my place, Nina. I can't reach up there and change them bulbs! So Ishmael is being nice enough to help me." Charly smiled, cunningly.

Nina fumed as Ishmael pulled up in front of her house. "Goodnight, girl," Charly sang. "Happy Easter!" Charly's smile was salt in Nina's wounds. Nina managed to say goodnight to the both of them as she stepped out of the truck and watched them drive off into the night. *'Fuckin' bitch! She always has a fuckin' trick up her sleeve.'* Nina stormed into her house, vowing that soon she would have a chance to get Ishmael's undivided attention.

But back in Ishmael's car, Charly was pulling out all the stops. As he maneuvered his truck down Myrtle Avenue. Ishmael listened to Charly filling him in on the frustration she was experiencing as she tried to find real love.

"Ishmael, I don't mean to be in your business or anything," Charly paused, long enough to have the dramatic effect she wanted. "But do you have a girl or a wife or anything like that?" She nonchalantly tossed her brown curls over her left shoulder as she awaited his response.

Ishmael shook his head. "Nah, I'm single right now. Why you wanna know?" He took his eyes off the road briefly and looked at her.

"I was curious, you know? I never knew of you being nobody's man. Every time I see you, you're with a different chick so I was curious if you've ever been in *love*."

Ishmael laughed. "In love? Damn, you're asking tough questions." He hesitated, hoping that the song on the radio would distract Charly from this topic of conversation. But not even DMX growling "What's My Name" could divert Charly's attention. "Yeah," Ishmael finally admitted. "I was in love once. A long time ago." Fearing she would want details, and knowing that the woman he had loved from afar had been Celeste, Ishmael flipped the script on Charly. "How about you? You ever been in love?"

Charly shrugged her shoulders. "Of course I have. But that shit is for the birds, you know what I'm saying? Love involves drama and giving another muthafucka power over your emotions and your happiness. I don't like relinquishing power to *nobody*." The look on Charly's face expressed that she was dead serious.

"I feel you, ma. Not too many women can help it, though," Ishmael explained. "Most of the time, if a woman goes into a situation with a nigga. They're trying to get to know each other and they could both say they're taking it slow. But in the long run, the nigga still sees it as just pussy and the woman done fell in love. Now she wants the nigga to stay and talk to her after they have sex, or she wants them to start spending more time together. Nine times out of ten, women catch feelings fast. So I'm surprised to hear you say that you ain't like that."

Charly looked at Ishmael. She thought, *'This nigga must think I'm an amateur. What kind of women has he been dealing with? They must be young girls that get sprung over some dick!'* She smiled.

"Well, don't be surprised, Ishmael. I bet I'm nothing at all like the bitches you fuck with."

They were at a red light on Morningstar Road. Ishmael turned and looked at Charly with a smirk on his face. "Really? What kind of bitches do you think I fuck with?"

Charly used her fingers to count off each point. "They ain't used to being with a nigga of your caliber. Most of the bitches you deal with are star struck. They're impressed by your status. They gotta be young. You don't want a woman my age…"

"How old are you?" Ishmael asked, as the light turned green and he made a left. Charly hesitated and

Ishmael tried to guess in his head as he made a right turn on Walker Street.

"Twenty nine. And I know that's not old, but you seem to like chicks between eighteen and twenty-one. At that age, women are still easily impressed. They have less experience in life and they fall for anything. And you're 31 so that means..."

"How you know how old I am?" Ishmael seemed genuinely flabbergasted by Charly's accuracy.

"The same way you know where I live." Charly smiled as Ishmael pulled up right in front of her house on Lake Avenue without her ever giving him directions. Before Ishmael could answer, Charly stepped out of the car and walked up the stairs to her front door. When she turned back towards Ishmael who was still seated behind the wheel of his truck, she summoned him with her finger in a "come here" motion. Ishmael put the truck in park and stepped out into the evening air. He followed Charly inside of her home and knew that he was not dealing with an amateur.

Sugar Walls

Charly locked her door once Ishmael stepped inside and she welcomed him into her playground. Her living room was dimly lit with amber hurricane lamps and her white leather sectional sealed the deal. She had well-polished hardwood floors and the room smelled like baby powder incense. Charly picked up the remote to her system and the radio came on playing a Jay Z song.

Ishmael stood near the doorway and looked around, took in the scene. Then he took his jacket off and laid it across the arm of the sofa and sat beside Charly. She crossed her legs and folded her arms across her chest.

"I'm not done with you yet." She said it so suggestively that Ishmael wasn't sure how he should respond. Lucky for him he took the safe route.

"Done with me? What did you start with me?"

Charly smiled. "I was telling you about the chicks you deal with. Those are the kinds of girls you like. And I'm nothing like those girls."

Ishmael nodded. "Yeah. I could tell by the conversation we just had." Ishmael looked her in the eye. "I can see that you do your homework, baby girl."

"When something arouses my interest, I look into it."

"So I got you aroused?" Ishmael licked his lips like he was ready for a snack.

"Nah," Charly said. "I said you aroused my *interest*."

Ishmael looked deflated and Charly smirked. "Obviously, I've aroused your interest as well. You had to do your own research to find out my exact home address. But I like your style, Ishmael. You come and go quietly."

"What about you? How do you come and go? What makes Charly tick?"

"Success," she said. "Success makes Charly tick. I have vision. I know what I want and I'm not afraid to go get it."

"Well what is it you're tryin' to get?" Ishmael looked a bit disinterested.

"Right now, I'm trying to get my car back." Charly was so sincere that Ishmael couldn't help but laugh.

"I feel you, girl. You'll get another one."

Charly nodded her head. "Yes, I will. You can bet your bottom dollar." Charlie's coffee table had double wood doors, which she opened and retrieved a pint of E&J Brandy. "You want a drink?" she asked.

Ishmael got comfortable. He nodded his head. "Yeah, I'll have a drink witchu, Charly."

Charly reached into her stash once more and retrieved two small glasses. She poured them both a drink and returned her bottle to its hiding place. Then Charly sat back and looked at the beautiful man sitting beside her. Physically beautiful, that is. He looked like a million bucks and Charly was yearning on the inside, while expressionless on the outside. She knew Ishmael was sizing her up as well. She looked good, and she smelled good and she knew it. Ishmael broke the silence as Charlie sipped her drink.

"So you got a man?"

"Nah."

"I find that hard to believe with you being this sexy. You live here alone?"

Charlie laughed. "Yup. Just me and my gat."

"What you need a gat for?" Ishmael couldn't understand why Charly's pretty ass would need a gun.

"Just in case I ever run into the big bad wolf or some shit."

Ishmael laughed. "What are you Little Red Riding Hood or somethin' now?"

Charly smiled. "Nah, more like Little Red ridin' *through* the hood!"

Ishmael was immediately impressed by Charly's quick wit and her sarcasm. He liked the way this was going. "Maybe the big bad wolf stole your car."

Charly licked her lips and laughed. "Well thank God I found someone as nice as you to drive me home."

"So how do I fit into the fairy tale?" he asked, his smile revealing dimples.

Charly returned his smile. "You're Prince Charming."

Ishmael nodded and took another sip. "Prince Charming, huh? I like that."

"What else you like?" she uncrossed her legs.

"I like *you*, baby girl."

"The feeling is mutual."

Ishmael inched closer. He leaned forward and kissed Charly and damn did she kiss like a champion. Her kisses were like liquid sex and Ishmael was instantly drawn in. Charly knew she had him. He slowly but surely started using his hands and they enveloped her breasts. Although she got soaked in the panties as soon as she felt his hands through her sweater, Charly pulled his hands away and continued to kiss him.

"Down, boy." She said it through clenched teeth as she playfully nibbled on Ishmael's lower lip. He was ready for whatever.

Charly continued to kiss Ishmael, and he continued exploring her body with his hands. He rubbed between her legs, pressing his hand up against the fabric of her sweatpants. Charly grinned. He smiled back and put his hands inside of her panties, toying with her clit. Charly couldn't help the enjoyment. She stared into Ishmael's eyes as he brought her close to orgasm. She stopped him, pulling his hand away and telling him to wait.

"Wait for what?" Ishmael was still pulling at her clothes playfully. Charly also smiled.

"I don't get down like that."

"Be quiet..."

Ishmael was laughing and so was Charly, but she was also serious. "I'm not fuckin' you, Ishmael."

"Why?"

"I'm just not."

"I'll change your mind."

Charly laughed and Ishmael tugged hard, pulling her pants off from her waist and over her ankles. Charly gasped but before she knew what happened, Ishmael had her panties pushed aside and his mouth on her clit. She was *instantly* submissive. He tongued her pussy the same way she had just kissed him. He was fully into it, and Charly watched him. He sucked and licked her so well. He sent her heart rate soaring and her defenses were down. Charly was gone. She couldn't believe the sensation she felt as Ishmael ate her like she was delicious. He continued to enjoy her until she couldn't help it. Charly came. And she was spent. Ishmael kissed slowly all the way up to Charly's breasts and undid her bra. She had the prettiest titties Ishmael had ever seen. Perky and full and he sucked on them. Charly was done resisting. He could have all the sex he wanted at that point. But his Nextel walkie-talkie phone interrupted.

"Yo, Ish! Niggas is shootin' at me..."

Ishmael wiped the wetness from his mouth, nose and chin and fumbled for his jacket. He retrieved his phone and talked to a very animated Rah-Lo. Charly tried to understand what was being said as she recovered from her orgasm.

"Who?" Ishmael demanded. "Where you at?"

"Where YOU at, nigga? I'm on my way to the spot. Meet me there now."

Their connection ceased and Ishmael grabbed his stuff. Looking at Charlie; naked from the waist down, with her slim waist exposed and her shirt lifted up over her bare breasts; Ishmael shook his head and wished he could hit it, just one good time. But he had no time. It sounded like a takeover was in the works and if Rah-Lo was being shot at, Ishmael had to help him shoot back. He kissed Charly on the lips and said, "We'll pick this up where we left off soon, baby girl."

Charly fixed her clothes and managed to walk Ishmael to the door. She locked it and watched him race off towards the bridge. Charly sipped her drink and she couldn't help smiling to herself. "I told him I wasn't fuckin' him."

The Hustler's Lair

Ishmael stepped into the basement apartment in Newark, New Jersey, and greeted all those assembled. This was Rah-Lo's uncle's basement. The place where the crew held their meetings was also the scene of many a heated encounter over the years. This was where the hustlers had their lair, and the meeting that was about to take place was sure to be a tense one. Rah-Lo sat in the center of the room flanked by J-Shawn and Harry on the left and Pappy on his right. Each one had been a crucial part of Rah-Lo's growth in the game.

J-Shawn was a friend of Rah-Lo's since high school, though the two had parted ways after they became adults. When word got out that Rah-Lo was doing big things, J-Shawn sought Rah-Lo out and told him that he wanted to be down with what Rah-Lo was doing. The two had been a team ever since.   To Rah-Lo, his bond with J-Shawn represented the time in his life when he was on top. He came into power at the point in his life that he was the most hungry.   He had a plan and a vision.   And it was so foolproof, so much of a sure thing, that J-Shawn wanted to be down.   Rah-Lo was proud of that phase in his life.   To him, that had been the turning point.   The point where he took stock of what he had lost versus what he could gain.

Harry was one of the knuckleheads that Rah-Lo grew up with in Park Hill. Harry was always in trouble, and had an itchy trigger finger. Folks from all the projects in Staten Island knew about Harry from the Hill and most resented him. The thing about Harry was that he was a trouble magnet. He always had been. His past included all kinds of crime, fights, shootouts, stabbings, and mayhem. Harry was a stick up kid. He would rob anybody – from old ladies with social security checks to elementary school students with allowance. Harry was only out for money and he would get it by any means necessary. But what was valuable about Harry was his connections. He knew all kinds of people – gangbangers, hit men, gunrunners, drug traffickers – and those kinds of connections are invaluable. There had been many occasions over the years where Harry's contacts had supplied the crew with artillery, or made witnesses disappear or somehow caused the tide to turn in their favor. Harry was Rah-Lo's go-to guy.

Pappy was a dust head. He was unpredictable at his best and a terror at his worst. He was the lethal weapon the crew kept in reserve. Their objective was to limit Pappy's violent shenanigans as much as possible. But that's hard to do when you're dealing with a dust head. Pappy was a live wire and his only real role was to be the muscle. He was also J-Shawn's cousin and that gave him the added familiarity.

Ishmael was the businessman in the crew. He knew all about every aspect of money – both legal and illegal. He was the plotter, the thinker, and Rah-Lo was the doer. Ishmael was the only one with a real job. He worked for a law firm, as ironic as that is. Ishmael was a mailroom employee at a reputable firm in Manhattan. His lifestyle in the streets would have been a shock to any of his co-workers, who knew Ishmael only as the quiet guy who worked hard and stayed low key. The importance of Ishmael's role in their crew could not be measured, since it was him who had the closest relationship with the leader – Rah-Lo. The two were childhood friends, both of them growing up in Brooklyn's notorious BedSty section. When Rah-Lo's mother moved him out to Staten Island in the eighth grade, Ishmael kept in touch. And as the years went by and the two grew up in parallel boroughs, they continued to have each other's back. Their friendship had endured for a lot of years, and it had helped Rah-Lo survive the loss of his mother. Before any major decisions were made about copping bricks or taking trips down south or anything of that nature, Rah-Lo always ran it past Ishmael. Sometimes, Ishmael felt that he was envied for his position. He never really hung with J-Shawn, Harry or Pappy. Those were Rah-Lo's friends. He only handled business with them and for the most part kept to himself.

The mood was rigid as he entered, and Ishmael sat in the corner, in the cut. Rah-Lo took the floor.

"Yo, muthafuckas from the Stapleton projects shot at me today," Rah-Lo said, astounded. "I can't believe them niggas got enough heart to do some shit like that." Rah-Lo knew that his name held a lot of weight in the street. He was big in Shaolin. Staten Island was where he laid his head, after all. But even outside the borough, Rah-Lo's name was synonymous with respect, and that type of respect was hard earned. He was a fair man; it wasn't unlike him to be generous or to lend a helping hand when needed. But when crossed, he was vicious. He couldn't fathom that anybody he knew in Stapleton would be bold enough to shoot at him. Except perhaps for one ignorant nigga named Jack.

"I believe it." J-Shawn spoke up. "Them streets are hungry. Whenever the have-nots outnumber the haves, anything's possible. Right now, all of us is caked up, living lavish, spendin' cheese. But the average Joe posted up on Broad Street...they ain't getting it like that."

"Plus niggas tried to rob my girl's shop today!" Rah-Lo yelled.

"You don't think them shootin' at you tonight had nothin' to do with Dre, right?" Harry asked. "Dre is from Stapleton, but I don't think he got the kind of power to have niggas shoot at you."

Rah-Lo shook his head. "Nah. I don't think Dre was important enough to cause a war on our crew. I think Jack and them Warren Street bullies shot at me today. But it all boils down to this. Muthafuckas no longer fear us in these streets. Niggas are going after my paper, my woman, my life. I ain't even gonna front. The shit got me looking at *everybody* funny. Even y'all niggas."

Silence blanketed the room.

Pappy spoke up. "Don't you think that's a bit much, Rah-Lo? Everybody in this room is part of the family."

"Yeah? Well where the fuck was the family when muthafuckas was bustin' at me?"

Harry shook his head. "Nigga, we was out getting money, just like you was. That's what we're all in business to do – get money. You're paranoid, Rah-Lo. Ain't nobody in this room tryin' to cut you out the picture. You know that. You're just shook right now…"

"I'm sayin', Harry. If somebody shot at you right after they tried to rob and rape your girl, you wouldn't be shook?" Every vein in Rah-Lo's neck was at attention. Harry nodded. "Of course I would. But that don't mean you got a reason to start suspecting niggas that been down with you since day one."

Ishmael nodded in agreement. "He's right, Ra. Nobody in here is out to get you. What we need to do is try and figure out why so many niggas got a death wish all of a sudden to start coming after you so hard. Something had to happen to make them feel untouchable."

Rah-Lo was heated. He paced the floor. "Whatever the fuck got them feelin' untouchable, they better think again. I'm about to start making examples out of muthafuckas. We'll see who feels untouchable after that."

Rah-Lo opened up a utility closet and briefly rummaged around. He stopped, and retrieved a piece of artillery that left the whole room speechless. Rah-Lo held in his hands a street sweeper, a weapon of mass destruction. "I'm going back to Stapleton. Them Broad Street niggas wanna bust their guns at me? I got somethin' for that ass."

Rah-Lo fished around in the utility closet for ammunition and the rest of his comrades also prepared for war. The first shots had already been fired. When it's on, it's on. Ishmael feared that the casualties would be great and the streets would be littered with crying mothers and fatherless children. He braced himself for the worst. Then he climbed behind the wheel of his truck and they all formed a four-car convoy. Destination? Stapleton.

Rah-Lo rode with Ishmael and he sat directly behind him in the back seat. His posture was reclined to the extreme. Ishmael also drove crouched down in his seat, his Kangol low over his eyes. He liked his hats like that. Situated just enough to see everything he needed to see. People often said things like, "I can't see your eyes." Or, "Can you see where you're going?" But that's how Ishmael liked it. He felt that they didn't need to see his eyes all the time. Just watch his style, watch his movements. And watch his gun go off.

Harry, with J-Shawn following him, took one route. After they all exited the expressway, the two of them followed Targee Street all the way to Broad Street. Ishmael drove the other way up Hill Street with Pappy following in his Land Cruiser. When they got close to the elementary school's playground on the corner, they crept up for a slow peek. The playground, which was bordered by a sizable parking lot, afforded them a good look at the block. It was busy. The night before Easter and all through the hood, folks was shopping and primping and looking real good. Everybody was posted up on the block. Ishmael looked at Rah-Lo through the rearview mirror. "Say the word."

Rah-Lo watched until Harry's blue Camry was visible on Broad Street. Seconds passed. "Let's get 'em."

Ishmael peeled a quick left and sped breakneck through the parking lot. He maneuvered the speed bumps until he came up in the back of the looming project building known as 212 Broad Street. Standing next to the black wrought iron fence, was Bones, a local tough guy who got his name from his lanky appearance. He was Dre's partner and he was guilty by association. Bones was standing, looking over his shoulder in the direction of Ishmael's squealing tires. Ishmael pulled up curbside and said. "Where Dre at?" Then he shot him, point blank, with a 12 gauge sawed off shotgun. The shot hit Bones in the chest and he was thrown back; hurled against the gate.

Anarchy erupted in Stapleton. The whole block was scattering. Everybody started running. Women with their hair wrapped in pins and scarves in preparation for church in the morning, dove for cover with their youngsters. Harry and J-Shawn came firing from the other direction of Broad Street. They littered the crews posted up in front of the bodegas and those standing outside of the project buildings as well, with bullets. Everything happened so fast that by the time Ishmael pulled off and hit the corner, Rah-Lo was already spraying the block with the street sweeper. Pappy was also shooting a cannon behind them and the shots echoed in Ishmael and Rah-Lo's ears. Harry spotted Jack, who was suspect number one. The only one who would have had enough guts to shoot at Rah-Lo hours earlier. He was the jive talkin' livewire who ran ounces for Neo. And at that moment, Jack was sprinting up the Broad Street walkway at top speed. Then, as Jack neared the middle of the straightaway, he shot back with his own two guns firing back at Rah-Lo and his crew. "I missed last time, nigga. But not this time!" Jack was actually laughing as he yelled over the gunfire.

Harry started busting at Jack and Jack was busting back. One gun in each hand, Jack was firing. Rah-Lo was almost out the window with the street sweeper, determined to lay Jack down. But J-Shawn fired the shot from his own Glock 9 that finally dropped Jack to his knees. One shot to the neck and Jack was down in mere seconds; sprawled on the pavement with screams and stampeding Timbs echoing all around him.

Sirens were only seconds away. Everybody in the crew sped off in different directions. Ishmael zipped up Van Duzer and headed for the Verrazano. Rah-Lo changed his clothes, concealed their weapons and climbed into the front seat. He lit one Newport after another, smoking to calm the adrenaline pumping through his veins. Neither of them spoke until they arrived in Newark, back in the basement of Rah-Lo's grandmother.

The Aftermath

"Muthafuckas get my drift now, you know what I'm sayin'?" Rah-Lo stated, plainly.

"Now they do.   Now they understand it ain't a game." Ishmael and Rah-Lo took turns guzzling a pint of Hennessy as they spoke. They were both still high off pure adrenalin, and now they compounded the effect with alcohol. Soon, Pappy arrived and the three of them were animated. They talked for a little while as they waited for Harry and J-Shawn. Nobody spoke after about twenty more minutes passed. Where were they? The once boisterous and amped up men stood silent. And that silence was deafening. It spoke volumes.

Rah-Lo's cell phone rang first. He talked to someone briefly, careful over every word he spoke on a telephone, and hung up. "Yo, this shit is crazy. Harry and J are both missing."

"Who was that on the phone?" Ishmael questioned.

"That was Charlene, Harry's girl. She said she heard about the shootout and she been calling Harry on his cell phone for the longest and she ain't get no answer. She thought maybe he got hurt or somethin'. She's worried about him."

"So now what?" Ishmael questioned.

"I wonder if the …" Rah-Lo never got to finish his sentence as Harry burst through the door. All conversation ceased momentarily. Finally, Ishmael broke the silence.

"What happened to you, nigga? Charlene said she been calling you. And where's J-Shawn."

Harry swigged the Hennessy that was passed to him. "I lost him after we left Stapleton. I laid low, stuck around Shaolin for a while to see if I heard from him. But the cops shut shit down quick and I had to get going."

"So where's J-Shawn?" Ishmael cut straight to the point.

"Good question. Word. I don't know the answer to that, though. I thought he would come straight here, but evidently, he had something better to do."

Silence again, as Harry continued sipping on the liquor.

"I don't know what's goin' on. But I know I'm laying the fuck low for a few days to see how it all plays out. I know that I did my part." He turned to Rah-Lo. "You saw that nigga hit the deck with a bullet to his neck, right?"

Rah-Lo nodded and gave Harry a pound. Harry passed the bottle to Rah-Lo. "Now all we gotta worry about is where J-Shawn went." Harry walked towards the door.

As he prepared to leave, Rah-Lo asked, "Where were you when you lost sight of J's car?"

"Headed for the expressway." Rah-Lo exchanged an understated glance with Ishmael and then Harry continued. "Since we all knew the plan, I figured he was on his way here. But I guess I was wrong."

Harry departed, leaving Ishmael, Rah-Lo and Pappy. Everybody needed time to come to grips with the events of the day. So one by one they all trailed off, exiting and heading for their own separate cars and destinations. Rah-Lo and Ishmael stood quiet in the driveway as Pappy departed. They looked at each other momentarily, both of them knowing that several scenarios could play out. J-Shawn was

missing. Where was he? From the expressway, J-Shawn
would have been at a sort of fork in the road. He could have
headed for the bridge to New Jersey or he could have made a
different move and gone back to Brooklyn. Or was he still in
Shaolin? They both smelled a rat. But they simply nodded
at each other. Ishmael's nod saying, "Yeah, somethin's
about to go down!" and Rah-Lo's saying, "Something went
wrong for real." Both of them wanted to know where the
hell J-Shawn was.

"If we don't hear from J within the next twenty four
hours, we got a problem." Ishmael said.

The two of them went off separately. As he drove
away, Rah-Lo was anxious to get home to Celeste so they
could help each other forget the events of the day. And for a
brief, fleeting moment, Ishmael contemplated calling Charly
for a do-over. But he chose to go home alone and atone,
instead.

Both Ishmael and Rah-Lo contemplated the rest of
their lives that night. They knew that something wasn't right.
J-Shawn was missing. Ishmael sat ready to take Rah-Lo's
lead. Without any verbal communications between them,
they both knew that they were at a fork in the road
themselves. Something big was about to go down.

Robin Hunter

Dime Piece was packed again. A day and a half had passed since the Broad Street massacre, and the fellas had been laying low. There had still been no word from J-Shawn and Rah-Lo was concerned to say the least. Celeste was concerned about Rah-Lo and the war he was waging in the mean streets. She loved him too much to survive if Rah-Lo was ever killed as a result of his lifestyle. He was her lifeline.

Celeste answered the phone, which rang continuously. *"Dime Piece*, can I help you?" She realized, with a sigh, that it was time for her to hire a receptionist to answer the phone in the shop. Celeste had too much other shit to do, for her to be stuck with a phone in her hand all day. The clients sang along to the radio, held their private conversations and sipped their coffee. All was calm, until Charly got started.

"Who was at my station, touching my shit? Where's the fuckin' Crème of Nature I just bought?"

Some of the clients snickered under their breath, while some cringed at the fire coming out of Charly's mouth.

"I'm sick of this shit! Y'all know when you're starting to run out of supplies. So go buy some! Stop using all mine. I shouldn't have to send somebody to the store every time I get a client just because y'all bitches ran out of relaxers!"

Nina shot back. "Bitch, you hardly ever *have* a client, so shut up. Don't nobody wanna hear all that mouth this early in the morning." Nina popped her gum and turned her back to Charly.

Charly put down the comb in her hand. "Excuse me? I don't hardly have clients, Nina? My chair is *rarely* empty. Unlike yours. And if you got so many clients, why you always begging Celeste to let you pay your rent late..."

"Ladies, no talking business in front of customers. I keep telling y'all that!" Celeste was tight, as she hung up the phone. Two unprofessional bitches! "And watch your language, we got kids in here!"

Nina seemed deaf to Celeste's warning. "Why you all in my business about when and if I pay my rent on time? As long as you pay yours, don't worry about mine. And, if I wanna use your relaxer and I got a customer in my chair while your shit is empty. Guess what? I'm gonna use that shit!"

The mother of the two little girls decided to take them to the store while the episode played out. No sense in exposing them to what would surely be a hellish face off. Now, the room was full of grown women. The clients started taking sides.

The woman sitting in Nina's chair, naturally, sided with Nina. "Charly, why you making such a big deal, anyway? You ain't even doing a relaxer right now."

Everyone looked at Charly's empty chair and wondered why she was causing a scene over a perm when she had no one's hair to do.

"Because the shit is mine. That's why."

Robin had heard enough. "Would y'all shut the fuck up, so I can concentrate? Some of us have work to do, you know?" A couple of 'ooh's and 'aah's erupted at the fact that Robin used profanity. She was supposed to be the quiet one. She was the low key one. Now she was getting just as hood as the rest of them. Celeste couldn't help but laugh.

Charly rolled her eyes at Robin and then set her sights back on Nina. "Buy your own things, Nina. With your broke ass!"

"Broke???" Nina seemed like she must have heard wrong? She put her hand on her forehead, and laid her scissors down on the workstation. Nina stepped out in front of her client's chair and went off. "Bitch, I KNOW you ain't talking about somebody being broke. I ain't nowhere near broke. I gets mine, you know what I'm saying? But I don't have to be on my back to do it. Unlike you. Guess what, Charly? If it wasn't for all the time you spent on your back and on your knees, your ass would be the definition of 'broke'."

Now the shop sounded like the audience at a boxing match. Everybody either laughed or commented, egging them on.

"What did she say?"

"Ooh, I know she ain't say that!"

"I would whoop her ass!"

"Look at Charly's face."

"Charly look mad as hell."

"All this over a relaxer!"

"It ain't about a relaxer no more," one of the older women under the dryer said. "Now it's personal."

Nina wasn't done. In a soft-spoken tone, she laid her cards on the table. "You got the nerve to say that I should buy my own shit. What have you bought for yourself, with your own money in the last year? I don't have to depend on *anybody*. You depend on *everybody*." Nina calmly folded her arms across her chest and looked at Charly antagonistically. "That's because you use your body to get what you have."

"Nina, who suck a dick better than you?" Charly laughed as she said it. "Who in town, Nina?" Loud laughter erupted from a few of the patrons and Celeste had to physically separate them after that one. Even Robin, who stood only 5'3" did her best to keep the two apart.

Charly was laughing as Celeste blocked her path. "Nina's jealous, ladies and gentleman. So she plays little third grade games. Stealing relaxers, saying all kinds of slick shit…It's okay, Nina. Don't worry. I know you wish you could live my life for just once. Hate all you want."

Charly grabbed her jacket off the coat rack. "Does anybody need supplies? I'm going to the hair supply store."

Celeste called Charly into her office and gave her a short list of things that were needed. She pleaded with Charly quietly to keep the peace. "You know Nina got issues, Charly…"

"So the fuck what, Celeste? Everybody got issues. Hers are gonna get her hurt one day."

"All I'm saying is that we all work together every day. For the time being that's just how it is. All of y'all got your own lives and you live 'em how you live 'em. Nina has a large clientele. So do you. There's gonna be jealousy and envy. Deal with it. But not in front of the customers."

Charly nodded and then walked back into the salon. She passed Nina at her station and walked by, smirking. Nina was scowling. Charly blew her a kiss as she walked outside.

Robin went back to her client. Nina was furious, and her client, Miss Pat, didn't like that one bit.

"Calm down before you do my hair!" Miss Pat said, adamantly.

So, Nina took a break and stood outside of the shop smoking a cigarette. Celeste couldn't believe the drama between Charly and Nina. She shook her head as she talked to Rah-Lo on the telephone. He told Celeste that he was sending Ishmael to the shop with a present for her to ease her mind. She hung up, wishing she could send him something to ease his own mind. He still hadn't heard from J-Shawn. He had simply disappeared. Rah-Lo and his boys were all on the edge of their seats, wondering where he went. And Celeste loved Rah-Lo so much that she wished she could somehow ease his mind. Despite all that, she sat anxiously anticipating Ishmael's arrival. Nina, meanwhile, was talking animatedly with her client and the shampoo girl. Charly soon came back from the store, walking past the women out front, and greeted her client who had finally arrived.

"I'm sorry I kept you waiting. We had a thief stealing supplies earlier." Charly ignored the scowls and glares from her coworkers and proceeded to cover her client with a cape. *"Dime Piece"* was emblazoned across the front of the cape and Celeste reminded herself that all the drama was worth it in order to keep her dream of ownership alive.

The Element of Surprise

By the time Charly walked her client to the sink in order to rinse her relaxer out, Ishmael was finally strolling in the door. He had his jacket kinda half on and half off, with it draped over just one arm and shoulder. Celeste was ready to burst with excitement, though she remained composed. "Wassup?" she said.

Ishmael laughed. "Stop trying to act all calm like you don't know I got something for you."

Celeste was all smiles as she led Ishmael through the back and into her office. Once inside, he opened his jacket to reveal a small Rottweiler puppy with a big green bow on it – her favorite color. The dog had a small folded handwritten note tied around its neck and she started to open it. But Ishmael wasn't done yet. "Don't read that in front of me and get all mushy and shit. There's one more thing." He dug into his pockets and retrieved a small box. Celeste opened it to reveal a pearl handled nine-millimeter handgun.

Ishmael nodded his approval. "Now that's a lady's gun," he said. "That shit is hot!"

Celeste smiled at Rah-Lo's ghetto love. She knew that this gun was to replace the one that had to be used in Dre's murder. This one was clean. Ishmael turned to leave as she opened the note.

I can't be there all the time. So for the times when I'm away, I got you a bark and a bite. I've taught you well. You're my better half. I love you.

Celeste was weak in the knees. She got right on the phone to call Rah-Lo and tell him how much she loved him.

Nina, in the meantime, watched as Ishmael made his way over to where Charly was putting her client under the dryer. "Good morning, Charly," Ishmael said with a smile. "I have a surprise for you as well." Charly seemed surprised. She handed her client a magazine and dried her hands on a paper towel.

"What you got for me, Ishmael?"

He beckoned her to follow him outside. They got to the curb and Ishmael walked her over to a Grand Am. "You can use this until you get your car back. I got a few connections, ya knawmean?"

Charly was shocked as he handed her the keys. But she noticed that he didn't say she could *have* the car. He said she could *use* it, until when? Charly read between the lines and decided the hidden meaning behind Ishmael's words. She assumed Ishmael meant until he wanted the shit back. "What's it gonna cost me?" she asked.

Ishmael smiled, showing his pearly whites. "Nah, I'm sayin'. For now, you know, you could use it free of charge. But depending on how long you need it, I could get you a good price for it." Ishmael put his hands in his pockets.

Charly would have preferred for him to give her the car indefinitely, but she saw that Ishmael had potential. "Word, Ishmael? Damn. That's wonderful. I appreciate that." Charly looked towards the front of the shop and noticed that Nina was conveniently smoking a cigarette, just feet from where they stood. Charly decided to give her something to see, with her nosy ass. "Ishmael, wow. I can't believe this!" Charly threw her arms around Ishmael's neck and kissed him sweetly on the cheek. "I appreciate this so much. You just don't know."

"I'm so glad I could help, ma." Ishmael moved in closer. "So when can I come pick up where we left off?" He was smiling and so was Charly. She knew that Nina was watching from the corner. She also knew that Ishmael wanted to claim his prize for the earth shattering orgasm he'd given her the other night.

"Well, let's get together tomorrow night. I'm off on Monday, so, I can hang out late that night." Ishmael nodded and they finalized the details. As he walked off toward his truck, Charly checked out the interior of her temporary new ride. She climbed out, locked it up and strode back to the front of the shop where Nina, Celeste and a client stood smoking and taking in the scene. Ishmael drove past slowly, so he could get a good look at Charly's ass in her jeans, and honked his horn. Charly (and all the other women) waved as he drove off.

"Funny how I get cars from niggas who ain't even got the pussy yet. That's why you hate. Right, Nina?"

Nina was jealous. It showed. "Any nigga that would buy you a car, would buy me a *house,*" she said.

"Whatever, precious,"Charly said, striding inside with the Nina close behind.

Both ladies resumed their posts at their stations. Celeste sat with her new puppy in her hands as a little girl petted him. "What are you going to name your dog?" the little girl asked.

Celeste shrugged. "I'll have to think about it." She looked at the puppy's sweet face and thought he was the cutest dog in the world. "Maybe Zeus."

Charly was applying her client's relaxer with gloved hands. "Yeah, that's a fly name. You know that dog is gonna get big, right?"

Nina interjected. "Of course it will, it's a rottweiler."

Charly threw a treacherous glare at Nina. "Wow. You know a little somethin'', huh?" Charly was being facetious as usual. Celeste's cell phone rang. She answered it and seemed fully engrossed in the conversation.

"What??" Celeste put her dog down on the floor and gave the caller her undivided attention. "How do you know?"

Robin continued braiding a client's hair at lightning speed while Celeste seemed disturbed by what her caller was saying. She started fishing around for her keys and packing her pocketbook.

"I'm on my way." Celeste flipped her cell phone closed and both Charly and Nina met her by the sinks, where Robin was already standing. Speaking in hushed tones, they discussed the situation. "J-Shawn called Rah-Lo claiming that he got kidnapped and now they want Rah-Lo to ante up." She shook her head. "I'm going to meet Rah-Lo so I'll be back before we close."

Celeste scooped up her puppy and departed. Nina and Charly avoided each other for the rest of the afternoon as the customers continued to arrive.

Celeste pulled up in her driveway and parked her truck. She walked up the steps, fiddling nervously with her keys to the large oak doors. But just as she reached the top step, Rah-Lo opened the door ushering her safely inside. She saw that Ishmael, Pappy and Harry were all assembled there as well. Her gaze lingered on Ishmael; he was looking better than ever. Celeste sat close beside her man on the sofa as he recounted the conversation with J-Shawn.

"The nigga sounded like he was under pressure. His voice was trembling and he was saying muthafuckas had him roped up. He said they want $100,000 or they're killing him."

"Who kidnapped him?" Celeste asked, with stress etched all over her face.

"Had to be Neo and them. We killed Jack and Jack worked for Neo. It has to be them." Ishmael surmised. "He didn't say for sure. I guess he couldn't say much or whatever. He just said that if we don't pay, he's a dead man."

"What if this is bullshit. How do we know J-Shawn ain't setting you up?" Pappy's criminal mind was at work. "Why are they only asking for a hundred grand?"

"When I was looking at y'all funny, wondering if I smelled a rat, I could have sworn you were the one telling me that this was a family. We all got each other's back, right? Well, why are you questioning J-Shawn's loyalty now?"

"I'm just saying. It took them damn near two days to tell us that they had him. Now they want this money by midnight. That shit sounds kinda suspect to me." Ishmael spoke up. "Well, the bottom line is, let's go see what's what and bring the money just in case this shit is for real."

Celeste felt like she was in a dream. Her mind was in a fog as she realized that this *was* all real. J-Shawn had been kidnapped, his life hung in the balance. Rah-Lo and Ishmael, Pappy and Harry were all preparing to put up most of what they had to bargain his life back. Or it could all be a set up – a trap used to snare Rah-Lo to be killed. Regardless, Rah-Lo set about gathering up the money. J-Shawn was in need, and it had to be dealt with. The other men left to do their part, while Celeste spent a few intimate hours with her love. At first, she held him, wanted him close to her to remind her that it was not his life hanging in the balance, but J-Shawn's. Celeste then kissed Rah-Lo hungrily until neither of them wanted to hold back any longer.

Rah-Lo was gentle with her as they made love. He took his time with her, caressing and kissing her softly. His brown skin laden with tattoos laid against her honey complexion, as they lay drenched in sweat. The spring warmth had little to do with this perspiration, though. There's was a physical heat. They were filling each other in all their empty spaces.

After they climaxed, the two of them lay spent. Then his phone rang disturbing their exhausted afterglow. Rah-Lo reached over and answered it. "Yo." He stroked Celeste body with his big rough and calloused hands. "So what you want me to do, Asia? I can't be everywhere at once."

Celeste rolled her eyes. Rah-Lo was a wonderful father, and Asia took advantage of that fact. It was during moments like this when Celeste and Rah-Lo were at their most intimate, when Asia always managed to call. To Celeste, that was another drawback to loving Rah-Lo. He came specially equipped with baby mama drama.

Rah-Lo slammed down the phone, furious that Asia was adding to his already soaring stress level. "She gets on my muthafuckin' nerves."

Celeste kissed Rah-Lo on his frowned up face. "Don't worry about it, now."

Rah-Lo sat up and reached over to the bedside table. He lit a Newport and rubbed his head in anguish. Celeste lay back against the numerous pillows, naked except for a thong. The bedside clock read 11:27, and Celeste could almost hear Rah-Lo's heart pounding. Harry and Pappy were making the drop with the money. They were hoping to pick up J-Shawn in the process. But it was risky. There was no telling who would be there to greet them when they arrived. Rah-Lo sat smoking repeated cigarettes, anxious for his cell phone to ring with an update.

He was tense, and so Celeste rubbed his back gently. Rah-Lo turned to Celeste and lay on top of her. She held on to him, ready to take his mind off of the situation at hand.

But then the door flew open and there were loud voices yelling, "TURN AROUND! PUT YOUR HANDS IN THE AIR!"

The Set Up

Celeste was naked in front of a room full of police officers in riot gear. Rah-Lo, clad in boxer shorts and socks, stood with his hands in the air, not saying anything. He looked at Celeste in a way that spoke silent paragraphs to her. The officers barked at her, not allowing her to put on some clothes. Rah-Lo was distraught that these men were seeing Celeste this vulnerable and naked. But his eyes told her what to do. *Don't say anything. Be strong. I got you. Don't worry. Don't say anything.*

Both Rah-Lo and Celeste were silent as they were made to lie facedown on the floor while the police searched Rah-Lo's home. They were helpless to do anything else and soon a female officer arrived and supervised Celeste getting. dressed. Then Celeste was handcuffed and led out to a police car. She looked out the passenger side window as she left Rah-Lo behind with a sprawling house full of police and uncertainty before him.

Meanwhile, down by the deserted naval barracks on Bay Street, Pappy and Harry stepped out of the black sedan and put the bag of money by the dumpster as agreed. They headed back to the car, waiting for a sign of J-Shawn and suddenly lights flooded the darkened area. "PUT YOUR HANDS IN THE AIR, YOU SON OF A BITCH! PUT EM UP!" Pappy and Harry did as they were told and submitted while they, too, were arrested. It was a setup, and they were all going down.

Celeste was promptly booked when she arrived at the police station and she was shown to a holding cell. It was a Tuesday evening, so the courts had closed for the night and Celeste was doomed to sit in limbo until morning. In the meantime, she called her mother. Celeste needed some help and she needed it fast.

To Celeste's surprise, her mother was out of town on business. Celeste elected not to tell her grandmother her predicament and she nervously thought of who else she could call. The thought occurred to her that Robin would still be at the shop waiting to lock up, so Celeste frantically dialed her number.

Robin answered on the third ring. *"Dime Piece*, may I help you?"

"Robin, it's me. Celeste. I need your help. I'm in jail…"

"For what?"

"For…I don't even know. It's a long story. Please get in touch with Ishmael. Tell him what happened. They got Rah-Lo, too. I need you to come to court in Staten Island and bail me out in the morning. I'll give you the details when you get here, just be at court in the morning. Tell Ishmael to be there, too."

Robin agreed to call Ishmael and she told Celeste that she would be there the next day. And she was. The following morning, Celeste was arraigned in Staten Island Criminal Court on Targee Street. She was charged as an accomplice in a long list of crimes. Rah-Lo, Harry, Pappy and Celeste were charged in connection with illegal gun and drug possession and Harry and Pappy were charged with drug trafficking. Since there were no drugs found – only the $100,000 in ransom money they were dropping off to get J-Shawn back – they were both hopeful that they could have that charge thrown out. It looked to the feds like a drug deal

gone wrong, when in fact it was an exchange in connection
with a kidnapping. But they would not explain that to the
cops. No snitching in the streets, that was rule number one.
They knew they had been set up. No way the police just
happened to be in position at the drop off spot. No way they
just happened to raid Rah-Lo's home that same night.
Someone on the inside had set them up. And once again,
Celeste was caught in the middle.

Robin sat in the third row of the courtroom with her
legs crossed, waiting for the court officers to call Celeste's
case. She looked at her watch once more and noticed that it
was almost 10am. She sat listening to the case of someone
arrested on breaking and entering in the projects on
Richmond Terrace. She sat across from Rah-Lo's wife,
Asia, looking troubled beyond words as she waited for her
husband to be arraigned. She wondered if Asia knew that
Rah-Lo had been arrested with his mistress, Celeste. Robin
couldn't help pitying herself and all the women who were
lured to men who lived this type of lifestyle. She shook her
head, frustrated by her own plight as a single mother since
Juno's murder. And now Celeste was languishing in a prison
cell and being subjected to God knows what, just for being
involved with a drug dealer. Ishmael entered the courtroom
and took a seat beside Robin. He couldn't help noticing that
her crossed legs were shapely and she looked strikingly
pretty so early in the morning. But Ishmael knew better than
to try and kick it to Robin. She was refined and was not the
type for casual sex. She was all about her son, and while
Robin did date occasionally, for the most part her main
concern was motherhood. And she made motherhood look
good.

"Good morning. How are you feeling?"

"Not so good until I know Celeste is alright."
Ishmael nodded his understanding.

"Celeste Styles!" The court officer barked her name
and she was ushered out with her hands shackled behind her

back. She glanced around the courtroom looking for Robin.
She spotted her sitting beside Ishmael and she breathed a
little easier, knowing that if bail was offered she might have
a shot at making it. She also noticed Asia staring coldly in
her direction and Celeste realized that the truth was out at
that point. The evil stare from Rah-Lo's wife let her know
that she knew all about them.

"Your honor, the defendant is the girlfriend of a
reputed drug kingpin. She was arrested in his home where
we found the two of them along with two nine-millimeter
handguns and a sawed off shotgun bearing no serial number.
The people ask that your honor hold the defendant without
bail."

Celeste's attorney spoke up. "Your honor, my client
is an upstanding member of the community. She is a
business owner and she is college educated. No illegal
substances or handguns were found on my client, and we
contend that she was simply in the wrong place at the wrong
time. She was merely a guest in her boyfriend's home at the
time of the police raid. Ms. Styles is not a flight risk and we
ask that you set bail at $25, 000."

The judge briefly reviewed Celeste's case and then
spoke. "Bail is set at $50,000." Celeste was ushered back to
the cell as she looked helplessly in the direction of Ishmael
and Robin. They both appeared reassuring. Ishmael winked
at her while Robin smiled warmly. Asia, seething from
jealousy and hatred towards Celeste, sat staring with an evil
in her eyes that was unmatched. Next to be arraigned was
Rah-Lo. He came out shackled at the wrist and at the ankles.
Knowing that Asia was in the courtroom, he did not look at
the spectators. His case was laid out.

"Your honor the people request that this defendant be
held without bail pending a grand jury investigation. The
defendant is the prime suspect in the murder of two suspects
on Broad Street several days ago. Seven other people were
injured, two critically, and the defendant's photo was picked

out by at least three witnesses. In addition, illegal guns and small amounts of marijuana were found on the defendant's premises and forensics is checking several packages of suspicious powder found as well."

"Your honor, my client maintains that the search was illegal and that he was never read his rights…"

The judge banged his gavel. "The defendant is remanded without bail." He arrogantly banged his gavel. "Next case," he said, arrogantly, banging his gavel again.

Rah-Lo didn't even look back as he was led away. It was the same story for Harry since a search of his home had turned up an arsenal of weapons. He, too, was denied bail. But Pappy was granted $100,000 bail. Robin looked hopelessly at Ishmael. "Now what?"

Ishmael shook his head. "We'll have to see. Let me try to get back to see Rah-Lo real quick. Then we'll make our next move."

Ishmael went to talk with the court officers while Robin went outside to use her cell phone. She called her babysitter, Miss Luke and checked up on Hezekiah. He was getting bigger and bigger each day. After confirming that her son was fine, she hung up. She stood outside the courthouse, sipping on a Dr. Pepper, wishing for the thousandth time that Juno, her son's father, was still alive. It would make things so much easier. This wasn't how she planned it. This wasn't how it was supposed to end up.

She thought back to the times when she was young, dumb and in love. She recalled all her mother's warnings, thought back on all the times she was told to be careful, to take her time growing up. She never listened. Robin had always been hard headed. She had to learn all her lessons the hard way. When he died, at Juno's funeral Robin learned several lessons the hard way. As Robin sat in her seat mourning the loss of the man she thought was her soul mate, several other grieving girlfriends of his showed up. Robin was almost ashamed as she rubbed her swollen belly,

watching one pretty girl after another break down at his side.
By the end of the day, Robin was too distraught and felt too
betrayed to attend the dinner his mother held at her home for
family and friends of the deceased. Robin wanted to stand
her ground. She wished she were brave enough to stand
proudly as the only woman that Juno had given his seed to.
She was, after all, the only one who would ever have his
child. But instead of feeling pride about that fact, Robin
couldn't help wondering if she had been the only woman
foolish enough to want that honor.

Ishmael emerged from the courthouse looking
despondent. He walked over to Robin and put his hands in
his pockets. "Rah-Lo knows he ain't coming home no time
soon. Neither is Harry. He said for us to do whatever
necessary to get Celeste out. So I'm going to handle that
now. I don't need what's in the safe since they set a
reasonable bail for her. We only have to put up a percentage
of that in cash, so I'll handle it. Pappy has his own paper so
he's gonna worry about his own bail money. You can go
and open the shop so that Celeste won't have to worry about
that when she gets out."

Robin nodded. "I'll go hold it down. I'll call Charly
and Nina and tell them to come in. Tell Celeste to go home.
I'll take care of *Dime Piece*. Don't worry."

Ishmael gave her a reassuring smile and she walked
off towards her car. She felt like she was in Celeste's shoes
momentarily. For a change, she was the one with the keys
headed to open up the shop. She imagined that it was *her*
shop she was going to, and Robin threw on her imitation
Chloe shades. She called them her "Zoë" shades as one of
her self-deprecating jokes. But for a little while she allowed
herself to imagine that she was running shit. She was the
one in charge, the one with a fat bank account and a fly car,
designer clothes, with power and respect. She lowered the
window and threw the volume up on her radio. She lip-
synced the words to Outkast's "Miss Jackson", and she felt

like a different woman. She found herself enjoying the role-play. And then she was saddened by the fact that it was only role-play. Robin wondered if she'd ever have all of that. Each day with Hezekiah made her want to rewind and get a do-over. But she felt guilty for feeling that way. After all, he was her son, and she loved him, unfailingly. It was for that reason that she worked hard towards a dream that even she was beginning to doubt would ever be a reality.

It's not that Robin had given up on her dreams. She couldn't. Being a good mother to her child was contingent upon her feeling like there was a light at the end of the tunnel. So she prayed that someday she would, in fact, have *all* the things she dreamed about. Including a good life for her child and a man to put the smile back on her face that she used to wear daily.

Robin neared the shop and came back to reality. She parked her car, bought a coffee from the coffee truck, walked to the shop and opened up for business. She was thankful that it was almost noon, since she was still worried after Celeste's attempted robbery. But the businesses on Lawrence Street were buzzing and patrons milled about. So Robin felt safe. She sipped her coffee and called the other stylists one by one to come in. Afterwards, she sat in her chair with her eyes closed and tried to go back to her wistful daydream. But as luck would have it, a customer walked in, wanting her hair styled in flat twists. Robin welcomed her in, and set about business as usual. Another day another dollar.

Nina Lords

J-Shawn's body was found on a rainy Monday morning about a week after Celeste's arrest. The corpse was found in an abandoned house on Brook Street. His arms were bound behind his back and his feet were also tied with rope. Duct tape covered the mouth on the decomposed face and it was an awful sight to see. Two bullets to the head. The whole crew was crushed. No one had yet been charged in the murder, but Rah-Lo and his boys knew for sure that it was Neo's doing. Word on the street was that he was responsible, both for J-Shawn's murder and for the police raid of Rah-Lo's home. It appeared that there had never been any hope for J-Shawn. They must have tortured Rah-Lo's address out of him before they murdered him. They killed him and then set the police hot on Rah-Lo and the crew's trail. The only thing that had saved Ishmael was that his role was to sit in the cut and wait to see who picked up the ransom money. Instead, Ishmael wound up with a front row seat as Pappy and Harry were surrounded and arrested. Ishmael managed to slip away in the midst of the melee.

Neo was the only one who cared enough about Jack and them Broad Street bullies to retaliate against J-Shawn so gruesomely. J-Shawn was dead and the whole crew had been set up. Everybody was under scrutiny. Celeste made bail, while Rah-Lo was being held indefinitely. Harry was still incarcerated as well. They put him in a different prison from Rah-Lo, though. Pappy, meanwhile, was being watched closely by the police. Ishmael on the other hand went about his business. A humble worker with a legitimate nine to five by day; a hungry man trying to make a million out of fifteen grand by night. He held the crew down and tried to keep a tight rein on Pappy.

Celeste was a mess without Rah-Lo to keep her sane. She continued to stay at his place in Shaolin. But she had to contend with Asia and her furor over the fact that Celeste had been revealed as Rah-Lo's mistress. Celeste had to change her phone number. All she received besides calls from Rah-Lo, were prank calls from an "anonymous" woman calling Celeste a bitch, a hoe and a home wrecker. And those were some of the PG-rated slurs. The phone at *Dime Piece* became a hotline for the same caller to hurl threats and obscenities at the woman who Asia felt was her only real competition for Rah-Lo's affection. Celeste began to spend a lot of time away from the close quarters of Staten Island. She spent a lot of time at the shop, busied herself with shopping sprees and visits to Rah-Lo. Celeste began to piece back together the life she had when she was single. The eight years with Rah-Lo, she had spent them bittersweetly. There had been more ups than downs, though, and Celeste continued to reap the rewards while Rah-Lo served his time. She redecorated the shop. Did the décor a vibrant red with whole new look. She installed a large screen television and nail station. On Friday and Saturday mornings, when the shop was most busy, they served doughnuts and coffee until noon. It was the toast of downtown Brooklyn before long. Their clientele was consistent because the shop was so comfortable and homey. The stylists were also expected to be consistent. But if an emergency happened, Celeste was understanding. She really treated them fairly and kept business mutually beneficial. But most of all, Nina was the most dependable.

She seemed to have a hunger for paper. If the shop was open on a Sunday or Monday which were their usual days off, Nina was always willing to come in. The girl was driven. She seemed determined to make as much money as possible and she did a damn good job. She was a very talented stylist and she seemed to do it so effortlessly. Her haircuts were always done with precision, her weaves always done so that no tracks or braids were visible. She was excellent at what she did. But it wasn't enough to make her feel contentment. Nina was determined to outshine her coworkers at all costs – particularly Charly. To her, working at *Dime Piece* was a competition and she refused to lose. To Nina, Celeste had chosen the best of the best and Nina wanted there to be no confusion as to who the star stylist was. It was about time that she got the attention she knew she deserved, and Nina would stop at nothing to have the spotlight all to herself for once in her life.

On a Saturday morning in May, a month after Rah-Lo's incarceration and J-Shawn's death, Celeste was stressed out and missing her man. She sat at her desk writing checks out to pay the bills and answering the constantly ringing phone. Robin was busy with a customer in her chair and four waiting to be braided. Nina was perfecting the blunt cut of a regular customer of hers. Her scissors moved with the grace of a dancer as the shampoo girl looked on, wishing she could cut hair with as much skill. The mood was calm, the customers sang along to the radio and the usual hustlers came in to sell their wares – cd's DVD's, slippers, bed sheets – you name it, they were selling it. It was a typical Saturday and many of the customers had been waiting hours for their turn. That was nothing extraordinary. The average client who arrived at nine a.m., was not finished until well after noon or one p.m. This was the norm in black beauty shops.

By the time Charly sashayed through the doors, it was after ten in the morning. Her clients had been waiting for over an hour, and they didn't know whether to be pissed off that they'd been kept waiting or relieved that she had finally arrived. She wore a radiant smile with her hair pulled back in a ponytail and just a touch of lip-gloss and mascara. Her jeans hugged every curve and the tank top was form fitting as well. It was all eyes on Charly and she loved it. Nina, in the meantime, was seething silently. Even the shampoo girl, who had been riveted by Nina's hair cutting technique, was now fully engrossed in what Charly was saying.

Charly tied the cape around her client's neck and began to cut the weave tracks out of her braided hair to prepare her for a shampoo. She started telling a story and soon her voice was the only sound that filled the shop other than the radio playing softly in the background. Charly was the center of attention.

"Ladies, I had the best time last night! I had a date with a guy I really like and it was off the hook!"

The customers were all ears. "Who's the guy, Charly? Ishmael?"

Charly smiled, coyly and avoided answering the question. "I'm not telling who it is. Just in case one of y'all bitches tries to steal him from me." Charly paused as the shop filled with laughter. "But I can tell you that he bought me these." Charly put her hands on her earlobes to accentuate the two-carat diamond studs that adorned them. Everyone gasped.

"Damn, girl! Those are so pretty."

"Charly! You must have really put it on that man!"

"Wow! Does this nigga have a brother? Or a father, cousin...something?"

Nina boiled internally. *'That's the only reason the bitch wore her hair pulled back today. She is such a show off. Ishmael is a damn fool for buying her those!'*

Celeste came over to inspect the merchandise. She knew that buying extravagant gifts for his women was not out of Ishmael's character. But she silently admired Charly for getting him to part with such an expensive gift after only a few weeks of them seeing each other. Charly was good, Celeste had to hand it to her.

Robin continued braiding her client's hair, but she smiled in Charly's direction. "Charly, I am scared of you! I give it a week before you have the matching tennis bracelet."

Charly and Robin gave each other a high five and the shop turned into a talk show audience.

"That's how you gotta have niggas!" one lady chimed in. "They will spend that money if they know they have to. You gotta show 'em that you expect to be treated like a queen."

Another client agreed. "Too many of these young, dumb girls are giving up the ass for nothing. Not even a meal at the McDonald's drive through! These stupid women are giving niggas head and taking backshots for FREE! Dumb bitches! Now Charly needs to round up about ten of those stupid broads and teach them how to run a nigga!"

"That's right!"

"You ain't lying, girl!"

"Mmmhmm!"

Charly smiled, pleased. Her client, sitting with her head to the side as Charly cut the weave out of her hair said, "I have never given up no free pussy."

"No romance without finance!" Charly agreed.

Nina rolled her eyes and handed her client a mirror to check out her new do. The woman was pleased and paid Nina, giving her a damn good tip. As Nina called her next client over to her chair, she listened to Charly lay out every detail of her date with Ishmael.

"See, he took me to Forty Deuce…"

"Where?" Old Miss Pat crossed her legs and leaned in closer.

"Times Square," Charly clarified. "We caught a flick, ate dinner at BBQ's and went back to his place. I talked to him for a while, you know. Then I let him kiss me a little, you know."

"Mmmhm. I know." Celeste said, grinning, slyly.

Charly's eyes danced at the memory. "I didn't give him *all* my goodies, though. I left him panting. When I woke up the next morning, his ass was in the kitchen making *me* breakfast."

Miss Pat held her hand up as if she was in church. She gave that 'amen' wave. "Now, THAT'S when you got a man right where you want his ass!" All the women in the shop erupted in unison like a choir and for a moment, you would have thought it was Sunday morning. Charly continued to testify.

"I didn't stress him. Didn't call him. I let him think about it. When I saw him again it was the weekend before my birthday."

"How convenient." Nina's sarcasm was evident.

"Well, call it what you want, but my ears are dripping in ice. Dripping!" Charly laughed at her own melodrama and walked her client to the sink. Robin's fingers moved at lightning speed through her customer's hair. The braids seemed perfectly even and precise. Celeste smiled, happy for Charly and her new ice. She went in the back to her office so that she could have a moment to think without all the talking going on in the shop.

War of Words

Nina began applying another relaxer – using her own products this time. She barely listened as the conversation continued about men and relationships. Nina was ready for her own Prince Charming. She wanted to be swept off her feet. She was tired of working. Nina had no family to speak of. Life on her own had been harder than most people knew. Abandoned by her father in her adolescence, and losing her mother to Cancer in her first year of adulthood, Nina was tired of feeling a void in her emotional life. She wanted the same kind of love that everyone else seemed to be enjoying. And why not? Why shouldn't she enjoy the company of a man who was after more than just some ass?

After her mother's death when Nina turned eighteen, she had no means of supporting herself. So she did what thousands of young girls before her had done. She turned to stripping. Nina's name was exotic enough that she didn't even bother to change it for the stage. She was a natural. She was a very uninhibited woman with a body that many women would envy. But the lifestyle of an exotic dancer was not what Nina wanted for herself. Nor was it what her mother would have wanted her to do. So in the daytime, Nina took classes at beautician school and quit stripping the day that she obtained her certificate. She felt better about herself now that she was doing something legit with her life.

But she still had some roads to cross before she felt complete.

And now, as she stood at the sink washing out her client's color rinse, Nina longed to be away from Charly's bragging ass for once. Nina wouldn't admit that what she was feeling was jealousy. To her, Charly was the problem. She was a show-off and she hogged the spotlight. It all made Nina sick. She found herself imagining that Ishmael had noticed *her* first, rather than Charly. She imagined what the look of envy on Charly's face would be like. Nina smiled at the thought and made up her mind to do whatever it took to take Charly's ego down a few notches. It was time for Nina to show her coworker how to be humble for once.

As if reading her mind, Charly sidled over to Nina and put her arm around her shoulder. "We should double date one night, Nina. Me and Ishmael. You and...well whoever. Let's do it one of these days." Charly walked away, switching her ample ass while Nina grinned connivingly.

"I can't wait," Nina replied, sarcastically.

They resumed their work just as Celeste emerged from her office. "Ladies, Robin will be locking up tonight. I'm on my way to see Rah-Lo." All the stylists voiced their agreement just as Ishmael walked in the door. He was driving Celeste upstate to Clinton Correctional Facility in Dannemora New York.

"Good morning, ladies. How's everybody doing today?" His voice sounded like music to Charly's ears and she fought the urge to run to him and kiss him with the same intensity she had the night prior. Ishmael smiled in her direction, and instead of running over to him, Charly gave him a subtle finger wave.

Nina watched the exchange and smiled inwardly. "Wassup, big spender?" Nina asked. Ishmael looked confused and then looked over at Charly. The earrings he gave her were gleaming in the light and he wondered if she had been in the shop telling their business. Ishmael didn't like his business in the street and now he wondered if messing with Charly was a smart move after all.

"Big spender? What's that supposed to mean?"

Charly looked at Nina with contempt and it only fueled Nina's fire. "Shit you must be friends with Jacob the Jeweler to get diamonds that clear!" Nina nodded her head in the direction of Charly and smiled at her. "Charly was telling us all about it. I'm jealous." She said it jokingly, but Charly recognized the truth in those words.

Ishmael looked heated. "Word? I knew my ears were ringing. Y'all was all in here talkin' about me? Wassup with that, Charly?" He looked in her direction.

Celeste stepped in to make the situation less tense. Every woman in the shop was watching to see if Ishmael would get mad at Celeste. "Please, Ish," Celeste said, dismissively. "You know how women talk in the hair salon. The same way y'all niggas talk shit in the barbershop."

Celeste laughed to lighten the mood, but Ishmael didn't reciprocate the gesture. "Come on, ma. You ready to go?"

Celeste nodded and grabbed her purse. She said goodbye to everyone and followed Ishmael out the door and they headed for his truck.

Charly wasted no time. "You fuckin' bitch! Why would you tell him what I was talking about?"

Nina smiled. "Why would *you* tell all of us your business if it was a secret. Let me find out Ishmael wants to keep you on the down low!"

The women in the shop shared a laugh at Charly's expense and it only made her angrier. "You know what your problem is, Nina? You are so fuckin' jealous of me..."

"Ain't nobody jealous of your hot ass, Charly. Trust me. I am happy being Nina."

"Why? What is there to be happy about? You ain't got no man, no family, no life whatsoever! What the hell is there for you to be happy about?"

Robin interjected. "Don't say shit like that, Charly. I don't why you two insist on arguing every goddamn week! The shit is ridiculous."

Nina tried to act as if Charly's jab about not having a family didn't hurt her. But it did. Rather than give Charly the benefit of knowing that it got to her, she smiled. "I don't want to argue with Charly," Nina said. "I just have a problem with people who seem *thirsty* for attention. Always gotta talk about themselves, always gotta have the spotlight on them, and every conversation gets twisted around so that the topic is them. Every time we start a conversation in here, it somehow winds up being a conversation about Charly. We could be talking about world peace. And Charly would find a way to turn that conversation around to focus on her." A few of the patrons silently nodded in agreement. "That shit is annoying. All I did was tell Ishmael that I liked the gift he got you. If it was a secret, you damn sure never should have put the shit on blast in the shop!"

Nina walked past Charly to the dryers located in the back, where she retrieved her client and led the woman back to her chair. Nina started to comb out the woman's wrap and she placed her curlers in the warming plate. Charly was so mad that Nina seemed unaffected by the stunt she'd just pulled, that she walked outside and lit a cigarette. The peanut gallery started buzzing as soon as the door closed behind her.

Robin's client was the first to speak up. "You know, Nina, you ain't lying about Charly being thirsty for attention. She is like that."

"She sure is," another woman said. "Every time I'm in here, she got another story to tell."

"Did you see the look on that guy's face when Nina told him what Charly said?"

"Word. He looked like he was pissed."

Nina nodded. "Wouldn't you be pissed if you spent a night with a nigga, bought him something nice and shit. And then you walk in the barbershop and find out that he was telling everybody about it? Shit, I would be pissed off, too!"

Robin played devil's advocate for a moment. "But, Nina, you do antagonize her sometimes. Every now and then you do something that enrages her, just to see her squirm. You start with her sometimes."

"Because I can't stand to be around somebody with an attitude like hers." Nina flipped the curlers skillfully through her client's hair.

"What makes y'all so different? You always look nice and dudes spend money on you, too," Robin said.

"But I keep my personal shit private and don't *want* people to envy me. That's the difference."

Charly strolled in just as she said it and looked menacingly in Nina's direction. She took a deep breath and resumed working on her client's hair. The radio was tuned to KISS since it was a cloudy day and nobody was in the mood for the heavy beats and upbeat tempo of hip hop. The song by the O-Jays came on. Everybody mouthed the words and some sang along loudly.

'What they do? They smile in your face... The backstabbers. Backstabbers.'

Kindred Spirits

Rah-Lo and Celeste sat across from one another at the table in the visiting room. He could almost feel the c.o.'s eyes staring at their table, waiting for something to set him off. They wanted Rah-Lo in the worst way; wanted his head on a platter. The guards couldn't stand him. He was respected and maybe even revered by most of his fellow inmates. But the guards couldn't stand the cocky and arrogant nigger who suddenly controlled the phone usage and television channels in the rec room. Rah-Lo went into prison knowing dudes who were already serving sentences. They embraced Rah-Lo and he naturally took the helm. He knew the guards watched his visits closely. So Ishmael escorted Celeste, but he never entered the facility or visited with Rah-Lo. It was bad enough that they watched him and Celeste so closely when she visited.

"What did your lawyer say?" Celeste asked. She had to fight the urge to hold him; had to remind herself not to make a spectacle. But damn she missed that man. He looked so handsome, like a rose growing from concrete. Celeste reached for his hand.

"He ain't say much, you know. They tryin' to get the charge thrown out and shit. We just gotta wait and see. I'm aiight. Knawmean?"

"Stop talkin' like that all the time," she said. "I'm not one of your boys, Rah-Lo. Just talk to me normal."

Rah-Lo looked at her like she was straight crazy. "What you mean 'talkin' like that'? Now all of a sudden you got a problem with the way I talk, Celeste? What's that about?"

Celeste shrugged. "I'm just saying that every time I ask you something, you're like 'knawmean' or 'I'm aiight'. That shit is annoying sometimes."

Rah-Lo told himself that Celeste must just be unusually testy. Maybe she was suffering from that PMS shit. "But what I don't understand is, when did my talking begin to annoy you?" Rah-Lo softened his tone. "What's the matter, mama? You pregnant or something?"

"Nah, you don't have to worry about that." Celeste regretted the words the minute she said it. Rah-Lo looked wounded when he heard her. Celeste tried to clean up the remark. "I'm just saying, you have enough to worry about with your case and J-Shawn being gone and everything."

Rah-Lo looked at Celeste wondering what had made her change. She was somehow different; somehow changed. This wasn't the Celeste that Rah-Lo knew and loved. Asia was usually the moody one. Celeste was always his sunshine. She seemed like she was at the end of her rope in their relationship. Rah-Lo wished he was home to fix what she was feeling. He knew that despite her love for him, Celeste wasn't one of the hood bitches like Asia was. Deep inside, Celeste was fragile, and the circumstances her life with Rah-Lo had put her in were also ones that had pushed her to the brink of their love. He wondered if she had what it took to hang in there and love him, whether he was walking crooked or straight.

"Ma, I know you ain't taking this shit well at all..."

"Hell, Rah-Lo. How am I supposed to take it?" Celeste released his hand. "I'm in that beautiful house with these beautiful clothes, a dog and a burner. Is that supposed to take your place?"

Rah-Lo was at a loss for words. He had a favor to ask of her and he felt terrible. He could already tell that his incarceration was troubling her and now he had to compound that turmoil as well. "I need you to take a break from coming up here for awhile. Asia wants to bring the girls up here to see me more often and I just don't want no trouble."

Celeste shook her head in dismay. "So I need to stay home alone while she comes up here so you can be one big happy family?"

"Nah, baby girl. I know how you feel..."

"Nah. You have no idea."

"ALL VISITS HAVE NOW ENDED!" the cracker c.o. barked the command as gruffly as he could. Celeste looked at Rah-Lo instantly regretting the fact that their time together had ended on that note. She hated leaving Rah-Lo with more weight in his shoulders than he had when she arrived.

"Baby, I love you. You know that," she said. "But I'm sick of living like this, Rah-Lo."

Rah-Lo hesitated before asking, "Are you gonna be waiting for me when I get out?"

Celeste closed her eyes and took a deep breath. "I'll be there when you come home." She kissed him goodbye and stood to leave. Rah-Lo hugged her close and then walked off towards the heavy doors. After retrieving all of her belongings from the prison's visiting room lockers, Celeste returned to the parking lot and climbed into the passenger seat of Ishmael's truck.

"How's he doin'?"

Celeste looked at Ishmael and frowned. "He's fine. I just wish I was." Celeste let out an exasperated sigh. "I'm sick of him being in jail, sick of coming up here to see him. This shit wasn't part of the plan, Ish."

Ishmael put the car in drive and headed toward New York City. "As his wifey, you have to be able to handle shit like this, Celeste. It might not have been part of the plan, but it was always a possibility."

"I'm not his wifey. Asia is."

Ishmael pulled no punches. "Well, you chose to accept that from the beginning. I could have told you a long time ago that you would get tired of playing second sooner or later."

Celeste chose not to respond and sat looking out the window at all the farms and cows they passed in upstate New York. The radio stations up there were obscure and Ishmael didn't bother to put on a cd. The silence was awkward so Celeste closed her eyes to get some sleep. Unfortunately for her, Ishmael wasn't letting her off that easily.

"Look at you. The truth hurts, huh?"

"Shut up. I know it comes with the territory. But that don't make it easy to deal with. You men act like we're supposed to just keep our chins up and ride. That shit ain't easy all the time. Yes, I have the material things and the luxury items. But I don't have the person in my life to complete the picture. That shit hurts and I don't think he realizes that. I know that I came into this relationship with both eyes open. I knew he was married. But I was dumb enough to think there would be a happy ending in all this."

Ishmael let the silence linger and he let Celeste vent. Then he spoke firmly. "Don't say 'you men' because we're not all the same. And don't say you're dumb because love makes everybody lose their senses."

She nodded. "You're right. It just seems funny hearing you give me advice about love."

"Why?"

"Cause you never seem to be in it. It seems like you pick women up and put them back down as quickly as you can."

"I know about love. I know enough to look at it logically."

Celeste sucked her teeth. "Please, Ishmael. This is me you're talking to."

"And? You can never say you've seen me handle my business the way you see most other hustlers handle theirs. I would rather not put my shorty in the position you're in right now."

Celeste laughed. "What shorty? You mean shorties right? Plural?"

Ishmael also laughed. "Well, that's just 'cause I'm looking for Miss Right. When I find her, I'll put all the other ones down." Celeste smiled and shrugged her shoulders.

"Maybe you will. Who am I to say?"

I'm telling you, ma. I live this lifestyle but this shit ain't who I am. God willing, I'll never be incarcerated for any lengthy amount of time. I do my shit smart. Keep a day job so they don't suspect you as quickly. The way I live my life is so unlike most of my counterparts. Most of them – pardon me for saying so, but even Rah-Lo – they eat and drink these streets. All they think about is how to come up in these streets. I want my story to have a happy ending, too. I don't want to do this shit forever."

Celeste nodded her understanding. She knew Ishmael well enough to know that he wasn't kicking dirt on Rah-Lo. The two of them had always been like Felix and Oscar. Rah-Lo was the wild one, while Ishmael took the low road. "That's good. More of your boys should think like you." What she wanted to say was that she wished Rah-Lo thought like him.

"Rah-Lo is lucky to have you by his side. A lot of women wouldn't care that he was away. He gave you the shop, he got you staying at his little mini mansion, your pockets are fat. A lot of women would be flashing right now. It's good to see you staying low key. It shows you got real love for Rah-Lo."

"I do. But I got no love for the game. And I got no love for the fact that he's married. I wish he had a plan to let it all go, but all he sees is today. There comes a point where you outgrow this shit."

Silence fell once more and they both fell into their own thoughts. Celeste smiled after a while and broke the silence. "So I'm still surprised that you got a soft side. The only side of you I've seen is the player."

Ishmael said, "When I find the one I'm looking for, I'll be the happiest man alive. Every young boy plays the field. But when you get to be a grown man, you gotta do grown man things. I'm ready to find my wifey. Ready to be a one woman man."

"Well, what kind of woman are you looking for, Ishmael? Someone like Charly?" Celeste wondered why she cared.

"Nah." Ishmael took his eyes off the steadily moving traffic momentarily. He looked at Celeste. "Actually, someone more like you."

Celeste felt her stomach go topsy-turvy and she wondered if she heard him right. He looked at her calmly and then turned his attention back to the traffic. She continued to look at Ishmael. For a fleeting moment, she wondered what would have happened if she had met him first. If she had met Ishmael before she met Rah-Lo. She wondered if the life she dreamed about would have been hers. Little did she know, Ishmael had the same thoughts. He had always thought Rah-Lo was lucky. He was lucky to have Celeste. But this was a line he would never cross and Ishmael almost wished he could take his words back.

The silence between them grew way too awkward, and Celeste sought to fill it with the radio. She fiddled with the dial until some old school R&B came on.

'Young hearts; run free; don't ever be hung up; hung up like my man and me...

Young hearts; to yourself be true; don't be a fool when; love really don't love you.'

Celeste closed her eyes and sang along to the words. Ishmael watched her affectionately. They both knew that no matter what could have been, they could never be more than friends.

A Day in the Life of Ishmael Wright

Standing in the doorway, his eyes couldn't move from the bounce in her booty. He didn't care who saw him looking. Her ass was something like a phenomenon.

She turned around and caught him looking. Smiling, Charly said, "Good morning, Ishmael."

He smiled back and licked his thick lips. "Good morning, beautiful." Ishmael didn't hold Charly's loose lips against her. He was too addicted to the other nice things she could do with her lips. She was a firecracker and Ishmael had fun with her. Her sex was satisfaction guaranteed. But once he found out that she was bragging, he stopped giving her things. He was a generous man who was raised to treat women like queens. So he showered them with little gifts just as he showered himself in nice things. It was just his way. But the last thing he, or any other man, wanted was to be perceived as a sucker.

So, Charly took it easy. She began to keep her love life to herself. But she was falling for him hard. There was something about Ishmael that was spellbinding. He talked to her and better yet, he listened. He was also thoughtful and he bought her things without her asking for them. As long as he was in her life, she felt safe and comfortable. And for the first time in her life, Charly felt that even without the glitz and the glamour, the money and the material things, she would still care for him. And for Charly, that was saying a lot. She had never been the type to want anything but a man with status. But as she got to know Ishmael, she liked the man so much more than just the status. Charly was falling in love.

Ishmael on the other hand, was just having a good time. He liked Charly. He admired her spunk and damn was she fine. But he wasn't in it for the long haul. He was having fun and taking it day by day. He never felt the need to verbalize that. After all, Charly wasn't like most women. She didn't act on her emotions like a lot of other women did. So Ishmael relaxed.

He stopped by the shop every now and then. He would always acknowledge Charly and the other girls. He would then spend most of his time with Celeste, making sure she was alright and that she never needed anything. He told himself that he was doing it for Rah-Lo. But as the months went by, and spring turned into a damn hot summer, Ishmael took great satisfaction in putting a smile on Celeste's face. He would take her for ice cream and they would laugh at private jokes. The two of them had a subtle flirting that was easily passed off as friendship. But Charly began to suspect something more. And it was then that she reared her ugly head.

It was a day in July, right after Independence Day. The shop had a moderate crowd, and one of the customers decided to make a run to Golden Krust for some beef patties. People placed their orders and Charly loudly requested a beef patty with cheese on coco bread. Ishmael and Celeste were in her office laughing at the Kings of Comedy DVD. The office door was open, and Nina went in there and told the two of them that someone was going to get lunch. Celeste placed her order and reached for her Coach bag to give up the money. Ishmael stopped her and pulled out a wad of cash. "You ain't gotta come out of your pocket when I'm around. You know that." Ishmael paid for Celeste's meal and that was that. But Charly, who was watching unnoticed just outside the office, boiled over.

She barged into the office. "Ishmael, you paying for mine, too?" she asked defiantly.

Celeste eyed Charly like her attitude was disgusting.

Ishmael frowned. "Didn't you already pay for your food?" he asked.

"Yes, she did, Ishmael. Don't pay her no mind." Nina walked out with the money and gave the orders to the girl headed out the front door. Charly was left standing in Celeste's office, feeling stupid and looking like a jealous bitch. She didn't know what to say except, "Let me get back to work."

"Good idea," Celeste said, sarcastically. Charly left closing the door halfway behind her. She went back to work, still mad that Ishmael and Celeste were so close.

Ishmael shook his head. "Yo, she be buggin' out sometimes. She's aiight and everything, but she started acting real possessive all of a sudden."

"That's cause she's getting that good lovin'", Celeste joked.

Ishmael didn't laugh. "Is that what you need?"

Celeste stared at Ishmael. The room was so still you could hear them breathing. Celeste didn't flinch. "Maybe it is."

Their faces were inches apart. Both of them wanted to kiss so badly they could taste it. A momentary lapse in self-control was cut short by Nina standing in the doorway. She cleared her throat. "Sorry to interrupt. Ishmael, the cops are gonna write you a ticket outside."

He stood up a little too quickly and put his hat on just over his eyes, and walked out, thanking Nina and leaving Celeste with egg on her face. Celeste struggled for an explanation, but Nina saw her struggle and cut her off.

"Girl, stop. Ain't nothing happen." Nina walked away, leaving Celeste thankful that Nina had been the one to stumble upon them and not Charly.

Outside, Ishmael explained to the ticket agent that he was just leaving. Nina walked outside the shop and strolled over to his car. "Can I get a ride to the beauty supply store on Jay Street?" she asked.

Ishmael obliged and she climbed into his truck. Charly fought to keep her mouth shut as she watched the scene unfold from her workstation. She watched through the window as Nina fastened her seatbelt, and Charly's eyes narrowed in contempt. Celeste emerged from her office just in time to see Ishmael pull off with Nina and Charly boiling in her Chanel sandals.

"You alright, Charly?" one perceptive customer asked.

"Yeah, girl. I am just fine." It would have sounded believable, if only Charly wasn't talking through clenched teeth.

"What's up, Ishmael? You look a little upset."

"Nah, I'm aiight. What's up witchu?" Ishmael wanted to know if Nina would talk about what she almost saw.

"I'm just doing my thing. I'm having a party tonight."

"Where?"

"At a supper club on Myrtle Ave. Quick's Lounge. You can come if you want." Nina paused. "That is, if Charly lets you come out tonight." Ishmael pulled up at the beauty supply store. He started to answer, but Nina jumped out of the car before he could do so. "I'll be right back," she said.

Ishmael waited patiently while Nina quickly purchased some weaving thread and bonding glue. She picked up some Razac and some neutralizing shampoo then she headed for the counter. When she got her change and receipt, she left and got back in the vehicle beside Ishmael. As soon as she put on her seatbelt, he began.

"First of all, nobody 'lets' me do anything. I'm a grown man."

Nina smiled, knowing he had thought about what she said.

He continued. "Second of all, you never even told me what kind of party it is. Is it your birthday or something?"

Ishmael drove and Nina shook her head. "It's just a party. I promote parties as kind of a side hustle. I have a lot of connections, so people come to network and have a good time. If you wanna come, you won't have to stand on line." Ishmael laughed at what she said. He never stood on line. He was too well connected to do something like that. He ignored the remark and kept driving.

"Well, thank you for the invitation. I might have my hands full this evening, but I'll keep it in mind for sure."

He pulled up in front of the shop and Nina waited for him to park. "Go'head, ma. I'm not coming back inside. I'll see you soon, though."

Nina winked at Ishmael and got out the car. He watched her walk to the shop and admired her sexy stride. He looked a little longer than he should have, and then he pulled away. Charly saw it all. Nina reentered the shop and placed her newly purchased items on her workstation. She ignored Charly's icy gazes and set about her tasks, smiling inwardly. Nina had planted the seed and decided to sit patiently and watch it grow.

True Colors

The shop was locked up, and Charly was in her car –
well, the car Ishmael loaned her – with her radio bumping,
and singing the words to Missy Elliot's hit. "Hot boys; baby
you got what I want." Charly was feeling better. When she
got over her initial anger, she realized that the women she
worked with were miserable. Celeste had been depressed
lately about Rah-Lo's situation and Asia's constant phone
calls. Nina seemed so lonely and boring. Robin was
struggling with her son, Hezekiah, and everyone seemed so
sad. But Charly had Ishmael, and he was someone she could
turn to take her away from the everyday. That was more
than any of the other women had at that point, and Charly
felt like she had the upper hand. That was how she liked it.
She was glad that she had Ishmael. She dialed his number
from her cell phone, inserting her earpiece in case the NYPD
was on the lookout that night. Ishmael answered on the third
ring.
　　"Whatup, ma?"
　　"Shit. What we doin' tonight?"
　　"You tell me, Charly. You seem to have all the
answers."
　　She frowned. "What's that supposed to mean?"
"I'm just saying, let me know what you wanna do."

Charly hated men and the word games they play. "I'm ridin' with you. You wanna go out, we can go out. If you're in for the night, I'm in for the night, baby." Charly softened her tone. She wanted to seduce Ishmael in the worst way. "I could imagine being *indoors* with you on a night like this. Wouldn't that be nice?"

Ishmael hesitated before answering. "Yeah. That would be nice. I'll be out to Shaolin in an hour or so."

Charly smiled and hung up the phone. She sang along with Alicia Keys all the way home. When she arrived, she straightened up the apartment and fixed her makeup. She always wanted to look nice for Ishmael. Charly put on the earrings he had given her and the bracelet to match, and she waited. When Ishmael arrived two and a half hours later, Charly was pissed.

She threw the door open and didn't bother to greet the man before she got started. "Damn. I thought you said an hour!"

Ishmael stood surprised and speechless. "Hello to you, too. What's your problem?" Ishmael walked past Charly and into the apartment.

She closed and locked the door and followed him. "My *problem* is that I hate to be kept waiting. Why tell me you'll be here in an hour and then show up two hours later?"

"I got caught up doing something..."

"Couldn't you call?"

Ishmael looked at Charly long and hard. Who the hell did she think she was? He took a deep breath, told himself not to flip out on the woman. "Yeah, I could have called. But I didn't."

"Then *that's* my problem. I need a man who feels that I'm important enough to call when he's going to be late." Charly put her hands on her hips and tilted her head to the side. She wasn't lying. Charly was used to having her way with men. Few had the guts to tell her no. She was a beautiful girl, but after seeing this side of her, Ishmael was beginning to think she was pretty ugly.

"I hope you find a man like that, Charly. Cause I'm not the one."

Charly seemed both hurt and surprised by his words. "What's that supposed to mean?"

Ishmael chuckled. "I'm not your man, remember? Weren't you the one saying that you don't get emotional and dramatic like other women do? You said, *'love is for the birds. Love is all about giving another muthafucka power over your emotions. I don't like relinquishing power to nobody.'* What happened to that?"

Charly cringed inwardly at the memory. *'Damn!'* she thought. *'He's good.'* But she wasn't going to let him win that easily. "Hold up. I never said I love you. This ain't about love."

"So why you acting like a woman in love? You want a phone call when I'm running late and all this. This shit was supposed to be fun, remember? This ain't fun no more. I walk in the door and you're barking at me..."

"Dogs bark, Ishmael."

"BITCHES BARK, CHARLY!"

Ishmael turned around and walked back out before he did or said something he would regret later on. Charly stood there livid and trying not to cry. Despite what she said, Ishmael had her all figured out. She was a woman in love.

He drove off and headed back to Brooklyn. He was on the expressway, bound for the Verrazano Bridge with his window down and the breeze clearing his mind. As he approached the exit that led to her place, he thought about Celeste. After he had driven her to visit Rah-Lo, he had promised to call her so that they could continue their discussion. He dialed her number on his cell phone.

"Hello?"

"Hey, you. It's Ishmael. What you doin'?"

Celeste exhaled when she heard his voice on the phone. He sounded as good as he looked with his baritone voice music to her ears. She wanted to hang up. Thoughts crossed Celeste's mind; about how unacceptable it was for her to talk to him about anything other than Rah-Lo. But still she found herself saying, "Hello. This call was unexpected."

"If it's a bad time to talk I could call you back," he said. "I'm man enough to admit that I just wanted to hear your voice."

Celeste smiled. She was glad they weren't face to face or he would have seen her blushing. "You seem to have a knack for saying all the right things. That's a little intimidating." She was surprised at her own straightforwardness.

He did not take long to respond. "Then maybe you're not used to someone saying all the right things. Maybe most dudes are saying all the wrong things."

"Maybe you're right. But how do manage to always be so charming?"

"You call it charm but I call it candor."

"But is it genuine?"

"It's quite sincere, Celeste."

Celeste hadn't enjoyed flirting so subtle and sensual in a long time. She found Ishmael to be a breath of fresh air in an otherwise suffocating existence. His conversations stimulated her mind and she realized how long she had been missing that.

But Celeste was also battling her own desires. As much as she was attracted to Ishmael; as much as she wanted his company, he was Rah-Lo's friend. Ishmael was her forbidden fruit in the Garden of Eden. "I was just on my way out," she lied.

He looked at the clock on his dashboard and frowned. "Where are you going at 11:57 at night?"

Celeste laughed. "Don't worry. I'm going over to Erin's house. She's upset and she said she needs to talk."

Ishmael's heart sank in disappointment. He was longing for her company. "Come on. Let me stop by for a minute."

As tempted as she was, Celeste stuck to her guns. "I can't, Ish. My friend needs me and I have to be there for her."

"Who's gonna be there for me?" Ishmael realized as soon as he said it, that those words came straight from his heart. He realized that perhaps it was for the best that Celeste was going out. The last thing he needed was to be alone with her – in Rah-Lo's house no less – with all the thoughts he'd been having of her. She was quite a unique woman.

Celeste didn't speak her heart. Instead she said. "You're a big boy. You'll be alright."

They both hung up just as Ishmael neared the Verrazano Bridge.

Nina was looking as good as she felt. The party was packed, the dj was playing all the right music, and she was feeling a nice buzz from three rum and cokes. Nina was the center of attention in a body hugging black strapless dress. She looked stunning and she felt sexy. She mingled with some of her friends – a few of the girls who were either strippers or former strippers. Some of the partiers were music industry insiders. They were the ones casting girls in the next hip hop video or looking for the perfect model for some rapper's clothing line. Everyone was dressed to kill and having a good time. Nina smiled to herself, estimating that more than one hundred people were present and the door price was $10 per person. Sounded like she would soon have the money she needed to get herself a car.

She made her way over to the bar and ordered a rum and coke. As she stood waiting for the bartender to prepare her drink, she looked around taking in the scene. She noticed a few of the girls she used to dance with looked so much older than the last time she'd seen them. They seemed worn out by life and just looked used and haggard. Nina was glad that she had gotten out when she did. She didn't want to end up looking old and ugly like so many of her former colleagues.

The bartender slid her drink over to her and Nina handed him a ten-dollar bill. But the bartender waved it off. "The man at the end of the bar said this one's on him." The bartender nodded his chin in the direction of Nina's benefactor and she looked – only to find that Ishmael had come after all. She was instantly elated, though she hid it well. She raised her glass in his direction as a silent toast and then waited as he made his way over to where she stood. Nina's heart raced with each step closer. Ishmael made her wanna holla!

Chemistry

Ishmael picked up an empty stool on the way and brought it for her to sit down. Nina smiled and sat down with her legs crossed exposing a lot of well-toned thigh. Ishmael was glad he came, since Nina so easily took his mind off of everything else.

"You look very nice tonight." Ishmael paid the compliment as he sipped his beer, but he looked damn good himself.

Nina sipped her drink and then licked her lips ever so subtly. "Thanks, Ishmael. And thank you for the drink as well."

"No problem." He looked around the crowded room. "Your party was a success, I see."

"Yeah. I'm glad so many people came out tonight. What made you decide to come?"

Ishmael wondered why he had thought twice about coming. Nina seemed like a nice enough person. "My other plans fell through, so I remembered our conversation and stopped by."

Nina wondered if Charly was involved in the plans that fell through, but she didn't dare ask. Charly wasn't at her party. Ishmael was.

"So tell me, Ishmael. What's your story?" Nina asked the vague question and took another sip of her drink. Ishmael looked visibly baffled

"My story?"

"Yeah. You know...who is the real Ishmael? Are you the nine to five brother trying to stay afloat? Or are you the block-hugger who dreams that he'll be the first hustler to make it?"

Ishmael smiled. He liked her analogy. "I'm a little bit of both. See, I am the nine to five brother, but I don't have to worry about staying afloat because I got my life jacket – the streets. And I don't think I'm a block-hugger, since you rarely see me posted up on the block. But I do have dreams of making it, and I wouldn't be the first hustler to make it, either."

"What hustlers do you know that retire from the game? Y'all get used to that fast money and it's hard to walk away from it."

"I'm gonna do it. Trust me. I'll show you rather than tell you." Ishmael sipped his beer and looked around again. The crowd was elbow to elbow and everybody was dancing to LL's Cool J's "Doin' It" song. People sang along and the floor vibrated from the motion of all the people dancing. "You wanna dance?"

Nina was surprised he asked. But she quickly said yes. The two of them headed for the dance floor and Nina snapped her fingers and danced with Ishmael. He was fun to dance with, and to her surprise he was a real good dancer. After several minutes, the deejay switched to reggae. Ishmael pulled her close and they swayed in synchronicity, grinding as if their hips were magnetized. Nina pulled out all the stops and tried to freak him on the dance floor. But Ishmael wasn't having it. He gave it alright back to her because he loved to see her move. Nina was poetry in motion and Ishmael imagined her doing the same moves behind closed doors. And then the unthinkable happened.

The sound of a heavy impact and glass shattering attracted everyone's attention. Someone cracked a bottle over somebody's head and the whole bar scattered. People stood around looking at the guy who got hit, watching him stumble trying to recover. It seemed that the man with the bottle didn't like the way the victim was dancing with some woman. The victim, however, chose not to be a victim for long. He pulled out a gun and the music stopped. Everybody fled, including Nina and Ishmael, as the shots rang out. The shooter was still dazed and aiming wildly. In the melee, Nina twisted her heel running in her new stilettos and fell. Ishmael turned back for her, stopping other people who were fleeing the gunfire from stepping on Nina. One guy pushed Ishmael and Ishmael punched him in the face. The man hit Ishmael back, and as Nina struggled to her feet and kicked off her shoes, Ishmael and the aggressive stranger were tussling.

The crowd was still headed for various exits and no one knew where the shooter was. The gunfire had ceased and Nina didn't bother to look around for victims. Instead she took the one good shoe she had left and charged Ishmael's opponent. She hit him right in the balls with the point of her shoe and he doubled over. Nina continued to hit him about the head and face as the man all but cried in agony from his groin. Ishmael pulled Nina off of him and dragged her toward the door. She fought Ishmael.

"Wait a minute. I gotta get my money for the party." Ishmael put her down and watched her run to the front where two men were separated from the crowd behind a glass enclosure. They opened the door for Nina and she entered, got her portion of the money from the party promoters and talked briefly with the men. She headed back to the front only to find that Ishmael was gone. She ran outside and saw him waiting in his truck with the engine running. Nina was relieved and she ran barefoot across the sidewalk to the truck and jumped in. Police cars arrived simultaneously, and cops ran inside the club with guns drawn.

"What kind of parties you be having?" Ishmael had a big gash on his head from his altercation at the party. Nina cringed when she saw it and suggested that he might need stitches.

"You should at least go to the emergency room and let them look at it…"

"I'm not going to the hospital tonight, man. I'll be there till Monday waiting for some doctor to see me." Ishmael shook his head defiantly as he drove. "And don't get me wrong, those shoes you had on are sexy as hell, but why do women buy shoes they can't run in?"

Nina rolled her eyes at Ishmael. "I didn't think I would have to run, Ishmael. I was supposed to be sexy tonight." She pouted. "My whole ankle twisted. That shit hurt. I had to sit there for a second 'cause I couldn't get up. How the hell did you get in a fight that fast?"

Ishmael kept his eyes on the road but he scowled as he told what happened. "The muthafucka was running out the club not caring if he was stepping on somebody. People get trampled like that. You were down on the floor looking like roadkill…"

"HEY!"

"I'm just saying, you was all sprawled out and shit." Ishmael tried not to laugh. "So, I tried to block the nigga from hurting you, knawmean. He gonna push me like 'move', so I punched that nigga in the face."

Nina shook her head at the adorable shoes she had just bought. Damn! The heel snapped like a twig. Ishmael continued driving and they both got lost in thought. Then Ishmael started laughing hysterically. Nina looked at him, wondering what the hell had tickled him so much. Ishmael really couldn't control his laughter as he drove. He was so hysterical that when they stopped at a red light, he put the car in park and continued laughing. Nina was annoyed now.

"What the fuck is so funny, Ishmael?"

He fought to control himself and then pulled off when the light turned green. "Why did you hit that man in the nuts like that, Nina? That was fucked up."

She tried to fight the smile that crept up on her face. But Nina couldn't help it, and she also burst out laughing. The two of them recalled together the look on the man's face when he felt the searing pain. "He wanted to cry so bad," Nina said.

Ishmael couldn't help but snicker. "As little as you are, with all that hostility in ya."

As Ishmael pulled up in front of Nina's house, she pretended to be mad that he was making fun of her. "Bring your silly self inside, please. I want to clean up that gash you got on your head."

Ishmael didn't hesitate to park the car and follow Nina to her walk up apartment. He rubbed his hands together, anticipating that she would show him just as good a time as Charly had. He smiled inwardly and followed her inside.

Next in Line

She let him in, and he looked around, immediately impressed by what he saw. Nina had sketchbooks all over the cherry wood antique coffee table. There was an easel near the window, and Nina had begun to draw the bench, swings and trees in the park across the street. She was gifted and Ishmael was impressed.

"Wow, ma, you did all this?" Ishmael stood admiring the drawings that were framed, and the ones spread out on the table.

Nina threw her purse on the black sectional, and shrugged off the question. "Yeah, I just do it for fun."

"You should do it for money, 'cause you're good." He held one up that looked like a little girl's silhouette. He admired her talent.

Nina smiled. "Thank you." She tossed her shoes in the corner. "Make yourself comfortable, I'm going to change."

Ishmael sat down and looked around. Nina was different from Charly. Charly was a flawless decorator. Everything was evenly themed, and her home had a classic characteristic about it. It looked expensive and so did she. Nina's place was earthy and feminine. She had antique furniture, like a record player with a needle, old school, with 45rpm records and albums from back in the day. Her walls weren't decked out in classy artwork like Charly's. Nina's were decorated with stenciling, and he wondered if she had done it herself. The pattern was similar to a henna tattoo all the way around the window. Nina had a different side to her, and Ishmael had to admit, he was intrigued.

She came back out wearing a tight yellow t-shirt and some black sweatpants. Ishmael was visibly disappointed. "Come on now, Nina, you were supposed to do it like in the movies. You were supposed to go in there and put on the little 'ling-er-ee', then you were supposed to come in here and seduce me." Ishmael was smiling, but he was only half-joking.

Nina chuckled. "I can see you've been hanging out with Charly." She said.

"What's that supposed to mean?"

Nina rolled her eyes again. "Please, you know exactly what I mean. I don't jump into things head-on like Charly does, I'd rather take my time."

Ishmael nodded, smiled. "Okay, I respect that."

Nina walked over towards him and was soon standing over him. She held a first aid kit and she cleaned his wound as best she could. To her, it didn't look so bad, after all. Ishmael smelled like almonds or cocoa butter. Nina bandaged his wound and closed up the kit, trying to avoid being sucked in by his scent. Then she sat beside him, with a safe distance between them. She picked up her remote control and turned the stereo on. She pressed play and her Musiq Soulchild cd came on.

Ishmael looked at her. She was a pretty girl, and even the frumpy clothes she was wearing, couldn't hide her sex appeal. "Why you sittin' all the way over there? I don't bite."

Nina moved closer. "Biting ain't always bad." She said.

Ishmael chuckled. "I like that." He watched Nina flex her pretty feet, apparently they were hurting her from her fall. "Feet hurt, huh?"

Nina shook her head. "That's not even the half of it. My ankle is killing me, I think I twisted it."

Ishmael reached out his hands. "Put it here."

Nina looked confused. "What?"

"Your foot, give it to me."

"What are you gonna do?"

"I ain't gonna hurt you, Nina."

"Promise?" Her eyes seemed like she was talking about more than just her foot.

Ishmael nodded. "I promise, ma. Gimme your foot."

Nina obliged and put her ankle in Ishmael's big, strong hands. He had nice hands, his nails were cut to a nice short length, and Nina didn't see any noticeable dirt under them. She watched as his fingers inched upward and cradled her ankle. Ishmael rubbed it gently at first to see if it was sore, then he applied a little pressure. Not too much, but just enough to loosen her tense muscle. Nina was so taken by him, that she closed her eyes, with a faint smile on her lips. "That feels nice." She said.

Ishmael smiled, happy that she was pleased. "I know it does, you fell pretty hard, ma." He continued to rub her ankle, and he thought back on how they had moved so fluidly together on the dance floor. He smiled at the recollection. "Where you learn how to dance like that, Nina? Damn, what are you a part time stripper or some shit?"

Nina opened her eyes and looked at Ishmael hard. She wondered if he knew more than she thought he did. But then she noticed that Ishmael was merely joking, asking a rhetorical question. Nina decided to blow his mind.

"Actually, I was a stripper once," she said.

Ishmael stopped rubbing immediately. "Word?" He folded his arms across his chest. Nina thought to herself,

- 115 -

'I guess my foot rub is over.' She sized up his response. He was playing it easy, trying not to look too surprised, but Nina could tell that he was.

She nodded slowly. "I had to do what I had to do, but I don't do those things anymore."

Ishmael nodded as well. "I respect your honesty. Really, that's a wonderful quality to have."

Nina grinned. "Thanks."

"May I ask what put you in a situation like that?"

She hesitated before answering. He had phrased the question interestingly. She wondered what it had been that put her in that place at that time. Was it the projects she grew up in, fast and acting grown? Was it the fact that her mother died before she turned nineteen? The fact that she felt abandoned by her father? She wondered how best to answer the question before her.

"I was young and on my own. I was broke, and women friends don't always have your back when you're down and out, so I did what I did. I'm not proud of that."

Ishmael was looking in her eyes. "I understand that, but why were you young and on your own?"

"You sure ask a lot of questions." Nina felt a little uneasy.

"Yeah, well, I'm just trying to get to know you, that's all."

"Let me get to know you, too. Tell me one of your deep dark secrets, I told you one of mine."

Ishmael thought about it. "I don't really keep no secrets."

What kind of things make you cry?"

"I don't really cry too much."

"When was the last time you cried?"

Ishmael looked at Nina, as he thought about it. Now, she was asking a lot of questions, and she was asking some hard ones, too. "About a year ago."

"What happened?" Nina batted her long, innocent-looking eyelashes.

Ishmael looked at Nina long and hard, wondering if he should be as honest as she had been. He looked away, and started rubbing her ankle again. Then he took a deep breath. "I lost somebody close to me, somebody I cared about, they got killed."

Nina was sympathetic, since she knew just how that felt. She missed her mother so much that she tried not to think about her often, because it was painful. Her curiosity got the best of her. "Who was it?"

"My sister." Nina was surprised. Ishmael stopped rubbing her ankle, and Nina thanked him as she withdrew her foot and sat upright.

"Who would kill your sister?"

"Her boyfriend. It was some love/hate shit, I guess." Ishmael's mind wandered, and he could still remember her face. His sister, Tangela, had been a sweet and impressionable girl, with ambition and a strong presence, just like Ishmael's. Unfortunately, to a man with a low self-image and animosity towards women, that strong presence proved to be a reason for him to kill her.

Nina and Ishmael sat quietly listening to Musiq. Ishmael broke the silence. "So, now back to your stripping."

Nina laughed and so did he. The awkwardness had been broken, and they both seemed relieved. With the tension lifted, they switched to the radio and listened to KISS. The deejay was playing old school R&B, and Nina and Ishmael got to know one another. They discussed their pasts, and then the conversation drifted to the present.

"So how did you wind up doing hair?" Ishmael asked.

"I was always good at it. When I had enough of the dancing, I put my other talents to good use and started styling. Then I met Celeste, and then I met you."

Ishmael liked how she summed it up so neatly. He had a feeling there had been more twists and turns than that, he would dig deeper later. Nina's phone rang, and she spoke briefly with someone and hung up.

"That was one of the promoters. They arrested the guy that shot up the place. He said two people got shot, but only in the leg or arm. They'll survive, thank God."

Ishmael shook his head. "You know how niggas get in the club."

"Yeah, I do." Nina knew all too well. "What made you turn to a life of crime?"

Ishmael laughed, again impressed by her wit. "Greed."

"That's one of the deadly sins, you know?"
"Yeah, I know. I'm working on it."

Nina smiled, she liked Ishmael a lot. He seemed like there was more to him than what floated on the surface. His waters flowed deeper and she wanted to dive in, but she reminded herself to take it slow. They talked all night, and when dawn threatened to peek through the curtains, Ishmael leaned close to Nina. Their lips were inches apart and he said, "You are so pretty."

"Thank you." She answered him, smiling. He kissed her, and his lips felt marvelous, and Nina wanted more. His tongue was sweet as cotton candy and he stroked her pretty, long hair. Their kiss was decadent, then Ishmael pulled away.

"Damn. I could kiss you all night." Ishmael was smiling. "There's something about you, Nina." He shook his head, trying to clear his mind. "Thank you for fixing me up."

Nina looked confused, and Ishmael pointed to his bandaged forehead. "Oh." She said. "You're welcome. I'm sorry the party got shot up and we couldn't finish getting our dance on, I was about to put it on you."

Ishmael raised his eyebrows. "It ain't too late for you to put it on me, now." Nina laughed and kissed his lips softly.

"Goodnight, Ishmael."

He smiled. "Ai'ight. Goodnight, Nina."

She walked him to the door and he walked out. She smiled to herself, feeling like a teenaged girl with a crush on the captain of the football team. Nina had to laugh to herself, because her life had never been the stuff that dreams are made of, but when she was with Ishmael, shit didn't seem so bad after all.

Ishmael drove away, feeling like he got to know Nina a little better than he expected to. He had honestly expected to sleep with her that night, but, strangely, he wasn't disappointed. His conversation with Nina had stimulated him for hours. And, after dealing with so many sharks in the streets, Nina's honesty was a breath of fresh air. Ishmael thought to himself, that the night hadn't gone so badly after all. Charly was a handful, and Ishmael decided that he wouldn't deal with her anymore. But Nina, she just might have potential.

Quiet Girls/Wild Girls

Dime Piece was packed.   There were so many
customers, that Celeste broke with tradition, and took some
clients. She was working on a roller set, trying to hurry up,
so that she could start on the next client. Celeste had always
sought to limit the length of the customers' wait time. Some
had already been there since nine in the morning, and it was
now almost noon, and few of them had moved from their
seats.   Charly was late and so was Robin, so Nina and
Celeste, held the fort down.

Just before noon, Charly strolled in, looking anxious
about something.   She offered no explanation for her
lateness.   Instead she gave Celeste a pitiful look and simply
said, "I'm sorry, it won't happen again."

Charly set to work and tied her smock around her
waist. She called over the next client, just as Robin arrived.
Robin's demeanor was frazzled and scattered, her shirt was
buttoned wrong and her clothes didn't really match.   She
looked like she had a rough morning. Robin immediately
began to explain that she woke up late, her son threw up on
her, she had to change her clothes and his, and then drop him
off at the sitter before speeding to work. She also apologized
to Celeste, and called over her first client.   But, unlike
Charly's customer, Robin's was irate.

"I hate to start shit." The lady said. "But, black people are the hardest people to do business with. This shop opened at 9 a.m., and I'm *just* getting started at damn near noon, that shit is ridiculous. Why not take appointments? Wouldn't that make sense? But no, you all would rather have people sitting in here for an entire day, waiting for their turn. It don't make sense. Now, I'd be wrong if I said I don't want you to do my hair, right?"

Robin was not in the mood for complaints that day. After the morning she'd had, Robin didn't give a shit if the woman had been waiting for three days, rather than three hours. Robin was not about to let this woman send her blood pressure soaring. She put down the cape she held in her hands, and glared at the woman. "Excuse me? I already apologized for being late and keeping you waiting. If you're that tired of waiting, there's a salon down the block. You can go wait for them to braid your hair."

Celeste gasped audibly. The customer was indignant. "Well, fuck you, too, then!" She said, standing dumbfounded.

Robin was unfazed. "Have a nice day." She said, stepping past the client. "Who's next?" Robin asked, in the direction of the awestruck clients who were waiting for their turn. One woman was making a beeline for Robin's chair, when Celeste finally stepped in.

"Robin can I talk to you in my office, please?"

Charly smirked and snickered at Robin's expense. It was obvious that Celeste was about to give Robin a thorough tongue-lashing. Charly found great amusement in that, the quiet one was finally getting her turn on the hot seat. Robin turned and looked at Charly when she heard her laughing.

"What's so funny, Charly? At least when I'm late, it's because I'm a mother. Usually when you're late, it's because you're a whore." Every customer in the shop burst out in laughter. Nina also laughed, louder than everybody else. Celeste took Robin by the arm and led her to her office, while Charly yelled behind her.

"That's what you need, Robin, a good stiff dick to take the stress out of your sad and lonely life!" Charly glared at Nina, who didn't bother to hide the smirk on her face. "Bitch!" Charly muttered.

"Yo mama!" Nina retorted, turning back to her client and whistling along with the radio.

Back in Celeste's office, Robin closed the door behind them, to block out Charly's annoying voice.

"Robin, what is wrong with you?" Celeste had a furrowed brow and a rigid stance as she looked at Robin, disappointingly. "You NEVER tell a client to go somewhere else to get their hair done. You know that!"

"She was being difficult, Celeste. If she knew what I went through to get here today, she wouldn't complain."

"That's not the point, the customer is always right. You *were* late. She has a right to be upset, but you NEVER suggest that a client take their money elsewhere. That's money out of my pocket and yours!" Robin stood silent and Celeste took a breath. "Take the rest of the day off."

"But I can't afford…"

Celeste cut Robin off by holding up several $50 bills. "Go home, Robin. Don't pick your son up from the babysitter yet, just go home and relax by yourself for once. You are overwhelmed. Go and get your mind right. Have a drink, take a bath. You need to do that for yourself. Then come back tomorrow feeling 100%."

Robin nodded, took the money and thanked Celeste. "I'm sorry," Robin said. I'm just feeling a lot of pressure right now."

Celeste smiled and nodded. "I understand, maybe Charly's suggestion wasn't such a bad one after all." Robin scowled at her and Celeste laughed. "Really, Robin, when's the last time you had your back dug out?"

Robin smiled half-heartedly. "It's been far too long." She admitted with a sigh. Then she turned and left for the day, as Celeste instructed her. Robin walked past Charly, giving her the finger on her way out.

"Use that to play with yourself, Robin. You'll be a happier person!"

Robin let the door slam as she left.

Heat

The heat was sweltering, and Robin walked two blocks to where she parked her car. She got inside and put the key in the ignition, but she engine did not start. The engine sputtered as she tried to start the car. She waited a few minutes and tried again. Nothing. Robin checked to make sure that she had gas, and that the battery wasn't dead. She couldn't find anything wrong. But, looking at the mileage on her car, she saw that there were well over 100,000 miles on the car. The car was on its last leg. Robin was beyond frustrated at that point. As if everything else that had gone wrong that day weren't enough, now her car had broken down! Robin pounded her head on the steering wheel in frustration and tried not to cry. She climbed out of the car and kicked one of the tires in frustration.

"Damn, looks like you're not having a good day." Robin turned to see Ishmael in his truck shaking his head and smiling at her. "Need a ride?" He asked.

Robin was relieved. She nodded and locked her hoopty, then climbed into Ishmael's truck. She was anxious to get home and rest as Celeste suggested. She gazed out the window as they pulled off.

"You are entirely too quiet." Ishmael said.

Robin rolled her eyes in exasperation. "I'm having a bad day. Please don't start with me."

Ishmael laughed. "My bad. I'm just saying that I would give anything to hear you scream just once!"

Robin knew that Ishmael didn't mean that comment in a sexual way, but that's exactly where her mind drifted once the words exited his mouth. Robin blushed from her own dirty mind, and Ishmael noticed.

"Get your mind out of the gutter." He said, smiling. "That's not the kind of screaming I was talking about."

Robin also smiled. "Well, you probably couldn't make me scream like *that* anyway." Her flirting was obvious. She licked her lips, and sized Ishmael up like he was a buffet and she was hungry. Although, Robin had never sweated Ishmael, she noticed that he looked damn good. And now that she was backed up, he was looking better than ever. He looked at her as if he wanted to meet her challenge, just as he pulled up in front of Robin's building.

Robin thanked Ishmael for the ride, and got ready to climb out of the car.

"You ain't gonna invite me inside?" He asked. He wasn't really joking, but he masked that fact by the smile on his face.

Robin rolled her eyes. "Anything you have to say to me, you can say right here, Ishmael."

He pressed a little further. "What if I don't want to say anything. What if I want to *do* something?"

Robin shrugged. "Do it."

Ishmael didn't need to be told twice. He leaned over and kissed Robin long and full. She let him, and before long, their hands were wandering, exploring the inside of one another's clothes. There was no turning back, so Robin pushed Ishmael away and climbed in the back seat. He smiled, intrigued by the quiet girl playing aggressive and leading the way to some action in the back seat of his jeep. Robin began to undress, and Ishmael pulled his truck over to the side of the building where there was little pedestrian traffic. Once he put the car in park, he followed her in the back, and sat down as Robin straddled him. Ishmael sucked on her breasts and she grinded on top of him.

"Give me a condom." She demanded. Ishmael fished in his pocket and found one, and watched Nina put it on him. When it was in place, she gave him head, that he knew would have felt better raw, but he wasn't complaining. When the condom was fully moist, Robin straddled Ishmael once more and it was on. She rode him right there in his truck in broad daylight, and he couldn't believe it. The fact alone that he was doing the nasty with Celeste's sensible and quiet employee – the one who seemed so innocent and young – almost sent him over the edge. He had to fight the urge to cum.

"Damn, Robin, where did this come from?"

"You want me to stop?" She asked, smiling.

"Nah, don't do that."

Within minutes, Robin had got herself off, and Ishmael wasn't far behind. It was crazy. They cleaned up, using paper towels in the back seat, and Ishmael sat in shock. He never really expected Robin to give him the panties. Ishmael guessed that what they said about quiet girls being wild girls was true. She climbed back into the front seat, and so did he. Without much more conversation, Robin thanked him for the ride, exited the truck and headed for her building. Her body was satisfied, and now she was focused on getting her car towed and repaired. Robin smiled, happily, as Ishmael honked the horn and pulled away. He smiled to himself, realizing that he had almost succeeded in sleeping with every one of the stylists at *Dime Piece*. He drove home to take a shower, feeling proud as a peacock. Now, all he had to do was conquer Nina. Two down, one to go.

What's Done in Darkness Comes to Light

Robin came to work the next day whistling a happy tune. Charly eyed her suspiciously, as Robin set up her work station, tied on her apron and called her first customer of the day. Robin smiled and greeted her client happily. Charly took it all in, so did Celeste, who smiled at Robin, wondering if she had taken her advice about getting a little "stress relief". Robin winked at Celeste, and nothing else needed to be said. Celeste smiled back at her and gave her a thumbs-up. Robin laughed at their private joke.

"What's with all the sign language?" Charly asked, looking from Robin to Celeste and back. "Let all of us in on the scoop!"

Robin shook her head. "Mind your business, Charly. This is grown folks stuff."

Nina laughed at Robin's jab, and switched over to the dryer to retrieve her client. Nina was looking exceptionally pretty that day. She wore a pale pink tube top with Baby Phat jeans that fit like a glove. Charly scowled at her and went back to work on the net weave she was doing. "Don't worry about it, Robin, I'm sure it was something boring, anyway!"

Robin couldn't help feeling vindicated. She had fucked Ishmael like he was the last man on earth, and Charly would die if she knew it. Robin saw no reason to let Charly know what they'd done. It was enough satisfaction that Robin knew how good Ishmael's sex was! It was a secret revenge for Charly getting on her last nerve the day before.

Robin walked past Nina and Nina grinned. "You got some didn't you?" Nina whispered so that Charly's nosy ass wouldn't hear them.

Robin fought back her smile, but it emerged triumphant regardless. She nodded vehemently. "Yeah, girl! It was the bomb, too!" Nina slapped her a high five and the two women giggled like schoolgirls.

"Who's the lucky guy? I know you put it on him, since you were in a drought for so damn long!"

Robin laughed. "I can't tell you. It's scandalous!"

Now, Nina really wanted to know. "I won't tell a soul, girl. You know you can trust me." Nina flashed her most innocent smile.

Robin caved in. "You better not tell anyone, especially Charly. She would have a fit."

Nina's heart sank even before Robin dropped the bomb.

"It was Ishmael! Damn, girl, his dick is so big!" Robin fanned herself as if she was burning up with heat from the memory. Nina tried to keep her game face on.

"Really? Girl, wow." Nina was speechless, but on the inside, she was crushed. She forced herself to keep her composure. "When? Where?"

Robin hung her head. "Girl, you would never believe me if I told you where, but it was yesterday and girl, he is no joke. I felt him all up in my spleen..."

"Where, Robin?" Nina had to know. She fought to keep her face from betraying her emotions; anger and disappointment.

Robin's bashful face gave way to a sexy smile. "Right in his truck, Nina!" Robin laughed. "Right in his truck in the middle of the day. I freaked him, had him frowned up, trying to hold back."

Robin even demonstrated with a hip swivel. Nina was jealous and disgusted, and she ended the conversation as quickly as possible. "Keep smiling, girl, it's good to see you happy."

Nina quickly returned to her workstation. She could hear people talking in animated conversation about the music industry, but Nina's mind was elsewhere. She couldn't believe that Ishmael was such a dog. Nina really liked him, and although she knew he was not her man, she was hurt.

Still nursing her wounded pride, Nina got back to work in a mood that was much more despondent than before. But, just as the conversation turned to the difference between real hip-hop and fake rap music, Ishmael walked in. Nina glared at him and then turned her client's chair around so that her back was facing the man who broke her heart.

Her actions didn't go unnoticed. Ishmael looked around for signs of trouble on the other girl's faces, but there were no telltale signals that would alert him to some bullshit. Charly waved and half-smiled. He knew she wanted him to come and talk to her in front of everybody. Robin played it low key and stayed towards the back of the shop. She waved at Ishmael, though. Nina, however, gave him no acknowledgment whatsoever. Celeste seized his attention.

"Hello, sir. How can we help you today?" She joked.

"Wow! Let me find out it's like that in here now," Ishmael said. "Ya'll trying to get upscale in the hood?"

Charly dove right in. "Ain't nothing wrong with bringing a little class to the gutter. You know what I mean?"

Ishmael smiled. "I think I do, but people throw the word 'class' around a lot these days." Ishmael watched Charly sewing a weave into a woman's cornrowed natural hair. He shook his head. "I love black women, but I can't stand them weaves."

Charly's eyes narrowed ever so slightly, as Ishmael's comment caused a major uproar. "What's wrong with a weave?" she asked.

Ishmael shook his head as he handed Celeste an envelope that Charly knew contained Rah-Lo's money. Celeste tucked it safely into her Dooney and Burke bag, and continued the conversation.

"Men talk all that shit about not liking weaves, but they love a woman with long, flowing hair. That's a double standard. Every time you turn on the TV., you see a light skinned woman with long hair parading around with these millionaires. You don't see a sister with an afro and a pick stuck inside of it."

Ishmael looked at her sideways as he walked slowly in Nina's direction. "Whatchu mean double standard? Weaves are fake. No man wants a fake woman. Black is beautiful. So let your blackness show. Stop trying to get all European and shit."

Celeste shook her head. "Whatever! Beyonce wears weaves, Lil Kim wears 'em, Mary, Eve, Faith, Toni. You're trying to tell me you wouldn't want to get with any of those women?"

Ishmael was now standing right in front of Nina. Even Nina herself, was caught off guard by how skillfully he had positioned himself there undetected. However, she avoided making eye contact with him.

"What about you, Nina? Your hair ain't fake. What do you think?" Ishmael stared at her intensely.

Nina kept styling. "I think as long as the woman's hair looks nice, it shouldn't matter if it's real or if it's fake. As long as the woman is real and not fake." She never looked directly at Ishmael.

Charly sucked her teeth loudly. "You are the poster child for 'fake'. Please!"

Nina stopped styling her client's hair. She looked at Charly, and thought she had to be the biggest hypocrite on the planet. Charly was the last person who should preach about getting one's act together. Then Nina looked at Ishmael, and she looked at him fully. This man, who was dangerously close with Celeste, who slept with Charly, and then fucked Robin in his truck. She was angry that she cared for him, and then she looked at Robin. The girl was nineteen years old, young and impressionable. Nina shook her head in dismay and walked outside.

Everyone watched as Nina walked outside and lit a cigarette. The only sound that was heard, was a casual conversation among the clients and the radio playing. Ishmael and Celeste both looked at Charly.

"What?" Charly asked, defensively. "The bitch is too sensitive. She can't handle the truth."

Celeste frowned. "You need to lay off that girl, Charly. Damn! Why you always hitting below the belt?"

"All's fair in love and war, right?" Charly said it to Celeste, but she was looking at Ishmael.

"You're something else, Charly." Ishmael said, and walked outside. He found Nina standing in quiet contemplation. Nina was trying to convince herself that she had somehow misread the signs. Ishmael was a dog, no matter how much she had enjoyed their conversation several nights before. No matter how candid he had been about his family, his past, himself, Nina told herself that it was all bullshit. Actions speak louder than words, she thought.

He stood beside her, wondering what was wrong with her. He could tell from his talk with her the other night, that Nina had a troubled past. He thought that Charly's remark and how it had wounded Nina's pride. What he didn't know was that what he'd done with Robin was the real reason for her blue mood.

"Why you letting Charly get to you?" Ishmael asked.

"It's not Charly that's bothering me."

"Who is?"

Nina fought the urge to say what she wanted to. "This job is, I want to go away from here."

"Where you wanna go, baby girl? I'll take you."

Nina looked at Ishmael cynically. "I don't want anybody to take me, I want to go on my own."

Ishmael held up his hands defensively. "Excuse me, I was just trying to help." He looked at her, trying to see if she was serious.

"You can go now." Nina flicked her cigarette butt into the street, and walked back inside. Ishmael stood for a moment, pretending not to be pissed that she had left him standing there. He wondered what the fuck her problem was. Instead of probing further, Ishmael calmly walked off towards his truck and went home.

The Hair I Wear

You say you love Black women but you can't stand weaves?

Brother that's not what you really believe!

If that's the case, I have a question or two

See the chicks that you pick are a reflection of you

Think back over the past few years and supply me

With an explanation for all the white girls and Boriqua mami's

Who you've chosen to play the role of your queen

Those chicks weren't spraying no Afro sheen

If you mean what you say about not liking weaves

Then your actions contradict your words it seems

Because most of the chicks brothers roll with these days

Are not dark skinned unless they work the runways

Do you send the correct message with the images you show

Of beauty defined by anorexic bimbos?

Why do you think that women in control

Like Lil Kim, Janet and Beyonce Knowles

Find it necessary to insert a few tracks on their dome?

It's because of the preferences brothers have shown

You say that Black is beautiful but you choose the European clones

You think Ashanti is finer than Angie Stone

I'll leave you with one last piece of information

Society never entered into my equation

Of how I choose to rock the hair that I wear

Whether you like it or not I really don't care

Because the hair on my head

I bought it

The tracks they sew in

I bought it

The glue is nice and tight

Cuz I bought it
And I depend on me.

What If Life Allowed Do-Overs?

Charly was done with her last client. She shut down her lights and curling irons at her station, and removed her smock. She checked herself one last time in the mirror, and was satisfied, after touching up her MAC lip-gloss, that she looked better than Mariah Carey and Jennifer Lopez combined. "Good night, everyone." She called.

Nina was almost done with her last client's short haircut, and didn't bother to say goodbye. Robin acknowledged Charly as she left, and Robin too, prepared to leave. "Nina, you need a ride?" She asked.

Nina shook her head quickly. "No thanks, I got a ride." She lied. The last person Nina wanted to ride home with was Robin. Having to hear about her exploits with Ishmael would just be more than she could handle.

Robin smiled. "With who?"

Celeste handed Nina the keys to the shop. "Don't let Robin get in your business, girl." Robin shared a laugh with Celeste. "Just lock up when your ride gets here." Celeste took Robin by the arm, and they walked out.

Nina was just brushing the hair off of her client and getting paid, when Ishmael walked in. She looked at him with contempt and thanked her client for her business. They were alone within moments.

"I came to drive you home," Ishmael said.

"I will never get in your car again, with your nasty ass." Nina couldn't help it. She had tried all day to keep her emotions in check. Now, it was late and she was tired, and her female counterparts were not around to enjoy her tirade, so she let go. Nina knew that she really had no other ride home, but she wasn't getting in his sexmobile.

Ishmael looked taken aback. "Wow, where did that come from?"

"Left field." Nina said, sarcastically. "I know my way home, and I can get there by myself."

Ishmael read her like a book. "So, you know about Robin, huh?"

Nina wanted to spit in his face. "Yeah, nigga, I know all about you now. Don't worry."

Ishmael saw that she was hurt, no matter how she tried to camouflage it. "Yo, that was just sex."

"Just don't worry about it."

"Nah, I'm worried about it."

"Don't worry about it."

"But I am."

"Don't."

"Would you let me speak?" Ishmael seemed exasperated. Nina was glad he was under pressure. "I just brought her home and..."

"Fucked her in your truck." Nina finished his sentence very matter-of-factly. "First, you were fucking Charly, and now Robin. What, am I next on the list?

"Nah."

"Then I'm not even on the list, huh?"

"I didn't say that."

"So, you really have a list, Ish?"

"Why are you twisting my words around?" Ishmael's shoulders were hunched and his eyebrows raised. "Come on, Nina, let me drive you home."

"I'm not riding in the truck you did that in." Nina turned off all the lights, and prepared to leave. "Go home, Ishmael."

"I want to go home with you."

"This ain't that type of party, Ishmael. Go call Charly. Better yet, call Robin. Maybe even Celeste."

"Hey, now!"

"Oh, excuse me, you're not *that* type of guy, huh?"

Nina stepped outside into the summer air, and waited for Ishmael to join her, so that she could lock the shop up. Ishmael looked at Nina, and instantly wondered if he had gone too far. By sleeping with Robin, had he ruined his chances with Nina? He hoped not, as he followed her outside and Nina locked up.

As she turned to leave, he took her by the arm. "Come on and let me drive you home. My head is still hurting from what happened at your party, and I want you to look at it. I might want to sue you or something." His humor was unwelcome and Nina turned from him. Chuck, the barber across the street, was locking up his shop as well and he saw Nina looking pretty in pink.

"You need a ride, ma?" Chuck called from across the street, hoping that the guy talking to Nina was not her man.

Nina smiled brightly. "Yes! Thanks, Chuck." She waved at Ishmael. "I got a ride, thanks. Have your people, call my people about your head injury."

She strutted fluidly across the street, and hopped into Chuck's Camry and they pulled away, leaving Ishmael standing alone on a crowded block.

Making Amends

The July heat was blazing, and the tempers in the shop were soaring like mercury in thermometers. Charly and Nina were at it again, but this time, the stakes were higher and the drama was at a fever pitch. Customers moved their chairs closer to the center of the salon, so they would have a birdseye view of the events unfolding.

"You know what, Nina? You can kiss my ass. I'm not even trying to hear you!" Charly turned and walked back to her station. Nina was right behind her.

"You stole my client, Charly!"

"I didn't steal shit."

"She came in here for a touch up, and when I went to the beauty supply store, you convinced her otherwise. By the time I got back, she was in your chair getting a weave. What kind of shit is that?"

Charly did entice the client, who had just left looking ravishing. The weave was perfect for the lady's face. "I don't see why you can't stand a little friendly competition, Nina. Get over it."

Nina tried to calm herself before she lunged at Charly. She didn't need to fight this girl and lose her job, so she stepped away from Charly, and narrowed her eyes. "You fuckin' bitch! You are the biggest troublemaker I have ever met in my life, I hate your stinkin' ass!"

"Awww." Charly purred antagonistically. "Hate is such a negative energy. Don't hate, congratulate."

Nina bit her lip and Celeste decided to intervene. "Nina and Charly, please. We're all making money today. There are plenty of customers waiting to be called." Celeste motioned towards the customers sitting in the front of the shop, patiently waiting their turn. "Let's go, no time for drama today."

Nina looked Charly up and down, and then walked away. Charly shook her head and said, "You shouldn't hate so hard, maybe Ishmael would notice you then." Charly snickered. Nina stopped in her tracks. "What's that supposed to mean?"

"Don't act like you don't know what I'm talking about. Every time Ishmael comes in here, you go out of your way to be noticed, and you go out of your way to talk to him. Anything he says, you agree with it, just to try and get his attention. He would notice you if you didn't try so hard to be like me." Charly was being paranoid.

Nina couldn't believe her ears. "Be like *you*? First of all, sweetie, I don't go out of my way to get anyone's attention. Second of all, I already had as much of Ishmael's attention as I wanted, and I had his *undivided* attention when I wanted it, too." Nina let her insinuation float in the atmosphere, as Charly squinted, trying to discern Nina's meaning.

'*She can't mean what I think she means.*' Charly studied Nina's face for some clue about what she meant. Nina simply smiled, winked at Charly and giggled. "Ishmael sure hasn't been checking for you lately, has he? Hmmm, I wonder why?" Nina put her index finger on her chin and gazed at the ceiling as if deep in thought. "I wonder why."

Even Celeste seemed surprised. She, too, wondered if Ishmael had slept with Nina. Inside, Celeste was somewhat envious. It seemed that no matter how much she and Ishmael wanted each other, he was determined to fuck every last one of her employees. The only one she didn't think he'd had yet was Robin, but Celeste wasn't even sure about that. She decided that when Ishmael arrived to take her upstate to see Rah-Lo that day, she would find out what was going on between him and all these women.

As if reading her thoughts, Ishmael entered the shop and greeted all those present. Nina ignored his presence, Charly scowled in his direction, and Robin winked at him. Ishmael decided that he didn't want too stay long. Things looked as if they could get ugly at any moment.

"Are you ready?" He asked Celeste.

She nodded, and went to her office to grab her purse. Ishmael wandered over to Nina's station and tried to engage her in conversation. "So, you made it home safe last night, I see."

Nina nodded and said nothing. Charly, meanwhile, was craning her neck, as she tried to listen to their discussion, that her intentions were obvious. Ishmael turned his back to her and lowered his voice.

"How about tonight? Do you want me to come back and get you?"

Nina shook her head, and said nothing.

"You really ain't gonna speak to me, huh?"

Charly had enough. "Stop sweating her, Ishmael. She didn't take her medication today."

Nina's jaw tensed and she got ready to let loose, but Ishmael came to her defense. "You know, Charly, every time I come in here, you got something to say about somebody. Do you ever get tired of hearing yourself talk?"

Charly was shocked and instantly embarrassed. Celeste agreed with Ishmael, as she came back out of her office. "She should, we're all pretty tired of hearing her clucking around here." Some of the clients laughed and Robin said, "Can't keep a chicken from clucking."

Charly started to speak up, but Ishmael cut her off. "I'll buy you whatever you want, if you promise to be seen and not heard for a whole twenty four hours."

Charly started to respond, but Ishmael interrupted. "Start now."

He walked out with Celeste, and the laughter of all the women in the shop behind him. Nina smiled to herself, grateful that Ishmael had handled Charly so that she didn't have to. Charly looked around at all the women, who she felt were just jealous of her beauty and style. "Fuck ya'll."

Robin couldn't hold back her laughter, and Nina joined her. Charly's face turned red and she turned up the volume on the radio to drown them out. They all made her sick!

Curiosity Killed the Cat

Celeste sat in the passenger seat singing along with Usher's "You Remind Me", as they headed upstate. She looked over at Ishmael, and it appeared that his mind was elsewhere.

"Penny for your thoughts." Celeste said, with a warm smile.

Ishmael snapped out of his thoughts and looked at Celeste. "Oh, my bad. I was just thinking about something I gotta do when I get back to Brooklyn."

Celeste only half-believed him. "No need to apologize. I just wanted to make sure that you weren't thinking about some chick while I'm sitting here looking as lovely as a summer day." Celeste was kidding, but she really didn't like the fact that Ishmael was spreading his love around Dime Piece. "Why you got them girls ready to kill each other over you?"

Ishmael feigned innocence, but the grin on his face gave him away. "I didn't do nothing, Charly's the problem."

"Did you have sex with Robin?" Celeste got right to the point.

Ishmael seemed surprised by the question. "Did she tell you that?"

"No, I'm just wondering."

He shook his head. "Nah." He was lying, but he looked sincere.

Celeste looked skeptical. She could see right through him. "Yes you did."

Ishmael laughed, and kept driving.

"Nina?" She asked.

He shook his head again. "Nah."

She watched for signs of deceit, but she found none and she believed him. "But you want to."

Ishmael looked at Celeste and frowned. "What makes you say that?"

"I can tell. It seems like you always try to get her to talk to you. You always show her lots of attention. But Charly seems like she gets on your nerves."

"She does. Her pussy was the bomb, but when she opens her mouth, it's a fuckin' turn off."

Celeste laughed. "Robin is sweet, but she's a mother, and I know you don't like women with kids."

Ishmael smiled, she knew him so well. "I wouldn't make her my girlfriend, but sex is another story."

"Just be careful. Robin is young, and she ain't ready for the kind of heartbreak you bring."

Ishmael frowned again. "I'm not a heartbreaker, I'm just an average guy."

Celeste made a face that said, *'Negro, please!'* "Ain't nothing average about you, Ish. I think you got it bad for Nina, though."

Ishmael didn't look at Celeste, he kept his eyes on the road. He wanted to say something, but he wasn't sure it was appropriate. Sensing his struggle, Celeste said, "Spit it out, Ishmael."

He glanced at her briefly, and then looked back at the traffic ahead of him. "I had it bad for *you* at one time." He admitted. "I don't want to disrespect Rah-Lo or nothing."

"Rah-Lo's not here." Celeste reminded him.

Ishmael nodded. "True. He's not, so I guess I can say what's on my mind, huh?'

She nodded.

He continued. "I was really feeling you for a minute. You seemed like the perfect woman, and I was so mad that Rah-Lo found you first. He already had Asia. That's his wife, so I felt like you would have been better off with me. I'm not proud to admit that I wanted you for myself. Rah-Lo's a good dude and I love him like a brother. He treats you right, and he loves you. He's a lucky man. So, I gotta find my perfect woman. Can't sit around wondering what could have been."

Silence cloaked them. Finally, Celeste spoke. "I know exactly how you feel."

They both got lost in thought, each of them wondering if they would have been a happy couple had things transpired differently. Celeste brought the conversation back to the situation at hand. "So, I guess you think Nina might be the one?"

Ishmael thought he detected a hint of jealousy in Celeste's tone, so he smiled and said, "She has potential. I like the fact that she don't feed into Charly's thirst for drama all the time. She could throw a lot of shit in Charly's face, but she don't do that."

Celeste hated hearing Ishmael speak so highly of Nina. She wanted to be the only woman in the shop who had an emotional connection to Ishmael, but Nina was threatening that. "Why's she mad at you?" Celeste asked. She had noticed Nina's cold treatment of Ishmael.

Ishmael grinned and looked away. "Cause I fucked Robin." He admitted.

Celeste couldn't help laughing. "I knew it, you are a man-whore."

Ishmael pretended to be offended. "Take that back."

"No, I mean that."

"You're gonna take that back before the day is over. Trust me."

They shared a laugh, and continued on their journey to visit the man they both felt loyalty to. Rah-Lo was the only thing that prevented Ishmael and Celeste from throwing caution to the wind and getting busy on the side of the Interstate.

After the visit was over, Celeste slept during the ride back. When they got back to *Dime Piece*, Ishmael reached over and woke her up. She stretched and yawned, got out of the car and followed Ishmael inside.

Charly cut her eyes at Ishmael, still salty about his earlier insults.   Charly continued putting the finishing touches on a blunt cut bob, and tried to avoid looking at Ishmael, but that was easier said than done. Robin had Ishmael engaged in a conversation, but Charly couldn't hear it since they spoke in hushed tones. Charly wondered if what Nina suggested had any truth to it. She wondered if Ishmael was grimy enough to sleep with her *and* her co-worker. Finished with his discussion with Robin, Ishmael turned back to Celeste and punched her playfully on the arm. Celeste smiled and he did it again.

"Stop, Ishmael!" Celeste protested, laughing. Ishmael grabbed her in a bear hug, and scooped Celeste up in the air.

"Take back the name you called me earlier." He insisted, as Celeste squealed amidst laughter and tried to wiggle free.

"No, I call 'em like I see 'em." Celeste refused to say that Ishmael was not a man-whore. Ishmael was laughing as well.

"Take it back, Celeste." His tone had a playful warning in it and he held her over his head.

Celeste gave in. "I take it back, damn!"

Ishmael put her down and Celeste slapped him hard on the arm. They both laughed, as did Robin, Nina and the two remaining clients, but Charly was livid. Celeste noticed immediately, but Ishmael seemed immune.

"Nina, you gonna let me take you home tonight?" Ishmael asked, with his heart-melting smile.

"Nope." Nina answered him matter-of-factly, and kept right on combing out her client's hair.

"Do you need a ride, Nina? I'll take you home," Robin offered. She was beginning to hate the way that Ishmael kept talking to Nina. She knew that what happened between her and Ishmael was nothing more than sex, but Robin couldn't help feeling cheap. Charly had gotten a car and diamonds out of Ishmael, but Robin hadn't gotten a thing. She had just asked Ishmael if he was coming to see her soon. His response ("We'll see") had made her feel quite low.

Nina shook her head. "Nah, I'm fine. Thanks for asking."

Ishmael shrugged his shoulders as if he gave up. He was getting tired of Nina acting like that. Part of him wondered why he even cared, but Celeste diverted his attention. "Nigga, go home. Thanks for the ride today." Celeste was also growing envious of the attention Ishmael gave Nina. She wasn't used to seeing him vie for the attention of any woman.

"You're kicking me out, woman?" Ishmael smiled. "I feel so used."

"Join the club." Robin said it under her breath as she left, but Celeste heard it, so did Nina. Charly was too busy scowling at Celeste to hear anything. Robin said farewell to everyone and exited.

Ishmael stuck around for a few minutes more, and then he, too, went home for the night. Charly glared at Celeste, but when Celeste looked up, and caught the expression on Charly's face, Charly looked away.

Celeste seemed surprised by the degree of venom Charly was silently spitting in her direction. "What's the matter with you, Charly?" She asked. Celeste addressed the situation head on.

Charly turned her back to Celeste, and handed her client the mirror to see her hairstyle. She had known her client, Miss Pat, for years. She was a longstanding client, so Charly let loose what she'd been holding back.

"Since you asked, Celeste, I'm gonna tell you." Charly put down her comb, and turned towards Celeste. Miss Pat got up out of the chair and stood near Nina and her client. Miss Pat (and everyone else there) was all ears. "Why do you insist on making a spectacle of yourself with Ishmael? You know what's going on between us, so why are you playing around like that?" Charly was angry, she had been with Ishmael first. All the other women had envied her, and now they wanted Ishmael for themselves, she thought.

Celeste just stared at Charly. Was the woman serious? "What is 'going on' between you and Ishmael, Charly? You fucked him, AND? SO! You fucked a lot of people. So has he, what makes you think I'm supposed to stop being friends with him because of that?"

Nina quickly got paid and sent her client packing. The young woman didn't leave though, she sat right there and watched the show.

"Friends is one thing, what you're doing is ridiculous. Every time he's talking to me about something, you're rushing him out the door." Charly said. "It's like you hate to see him give anybody attention except you. He's not your man."

Celeste laughed, incredulously. "When I do that, it's usually because he's putting your dumb ass down!"

Charly stepped closer to Celeste. "I'm *dumb*, Celeste? I'm just as smart as you are. That's why you're intimidated. It's okay, I'm used to that. You know, all you did was find the right man, you didn't accomplish this yourself." Charly motioned at the lovely salon in which they stood. "Rah-Lo's married so he has to keep you from leaving him by giving you these things. You didn't earn this shop. You got it just for being exactly what you named it, a dime piece. And guess what? You're not the only one, I'm a dime piece, too, Celeste. So, don't block what I got goin' on." Celeste said nothing, so Charly stepped in further. "I'm not the dumb one. Am I? Rah-Lo's the dumb one, for not seeing that his second wifey is damn near fucking his boy."

Celeste pounced. She lunged at Charly and smacked her face so hard that it echoed. Nina didn't intervene as they tussled. Instead, she stood back and watched Charly get her hits in, but Celeste beat Charly's ass. When it got to the point that Celeste had a handful of Charly's mid-back length weave, and was punching her square in the face, Nina stepped in. She grabbed Celeste by the arm and coaxed her to let Charly go.

"Come on now, girl. That's enough."

"You don't fuckin' tell me who to be friends with!" Celeste yelled at Charly. Nina's customer left and Miss Pat stood amazed. "You don't dictate how I act with my friends. You are a twisted little girl, Charly, and you need to grow up. You stupid bitch!" Celeste was fuming. Nina pulled her back and brought her over towards the door.

"Come on, Celeste, let's go. Don't waste your breath." Nina blocked Celeste's path as Miss Pat calmed Charly down. Charly was swollen and puffy, but she still had mouth.

"Fuck you, Celeste. You've been wanting to hit me ever since I started dealing with Ishmael. Do you feel better now? You jealous bitch."

"You're fired, dummy. Get your shit and get out."

"Kiss my ass. You can have my shit, that's how worthless you are. Rah-Lo better wake up, Celeste!" Charly was crying from anger and frustration. "He better open his eyes and see that his best friend is fucking his bitch. I hope somebody lets him know."

"Leave, Charly." Nina tried to say it sensibly, but Charly spit back.

"Your orphan ass need to sit down somewhere."

Nina smacked Charly hard, and she lunged at Nina. Miss Pat did her best to intervene, but not before she could stop her, Celeste punched Charly so hard, that Miss Pat threatened to call the cops if Celeste hit her like that again.

Charly talked shit all the way to the sidewalk, where Miss Pat tried her best to calm her. Charly looked a wreck, but she didn't back down. Celeste paced the floor, irate, while Nina listened to Charly spewing hate and negative energy.

"Watch what happens, Celeste. It's on now, bitch!"

Ride or Die?

By the time Celeste told Ishmael what happened, Charly had started working at the shop down the street. Ishmael was stunned. He couldn't believe Charly had gone that far, over what he thought was a casual relationship. He never expected her to start a fight over him; especially not with Celeste. Ishmael asked Celeste, point blank, if she could see herself leaving Rah-Lo. He felt he had nothing to lose since he wasn't asking her if she would leave Rah-Lo to be with him. Instead, he wondered if she would ever get tired of a love that made her feel second best.

Celeste pondered Ishmael's question and understood the significance of her response. Her answer would determine whether Ishmael continued to hold out hope for her. He could walk away forever, and Celeste wasn't sure she was ready for that. "I know that there's better out there for me, but I love him. He understands me on a level that nobody else ever has. Rah-Lo is the love of my life," she said. "I can't walk away until I feel that I've given it all that I got."

Ishmael was disappointed in her answer, though he accepted it. He felt that Celeste had already given her all in her relationship with Rah-Lo. She held a special place in Ishmael's heart and it pained him to admit to himself that it was time for him to get over his crush on Celeste. It was a lost cause. But he had more things on his mind than the drama among the women in his life.

Pappy found himself in trouble. Pappy was on the run after he got dusted and shot his stepfather. The man survived, but Pappy was in trouble, he was a wanted man. Ishmael helped him stay underground, but Pappy had a mind of his own. Ishmael knew it was only a matter of time before Pappy ended up dead either from an overdose or from pure karma. In the meantime, Rah-Lo was soon coming home, after getting some of the major charges against him thrown out on technicalities. But, Harry wasn't so lucky. He wouldn't snitch on those with whom he did business, and the arsenal they found in his home, was more than sizeable. He was looking at twenty-five years to life, on charges with substantial evidence to back them up. But Harry wouldn't snitch, and in the streets he was a hero for that.

So, Ishmael anticipated Rah-Lo's return. He also wondered if the sentiments Charly had expressed, were ones that might be echoed by others in their midst. He wondered if his relationship with Celeste had crossed an invisible boundary, despite his battle to avoid just that. Ishmael began to reexamine his relationship with Celeste before Rah-Lo came home. So, he stopped driving her upstate. He limited his trips to the shop, and when he did stop by, he came to see Nina. Ishmael was beginning to grow tired of the game playing. He was tiring of being a ladies man. He wanted a love like Rah-Lo had, and he was beginning to think he might find it with Nina.

Every night, she took the long walk home, rather than take a ride from Ishmael. It bothered him, despite his foolish pride telling him that it shouldn't. Ishmael was on the rise. He was holding down the fort in the street and the money was pouring in. Rah-Lo's cut was split between Asia and Celeste each time, but Ishmael was beginning to see more and more money. It was more than he had ever dreamed of having. He had been lucky. Rah-Lo was locked down, so was Harry. Pappy was on the run, and he felt like the last man standing. He had achieved success, and now all he needed was a woman to share it with.

One night in August, Nina had walked all the way home, and her "dogs" were barking by the time she reached her front door. Just as she put her hand on the doorknob, a horn honked behind her, and the surprise was evident on her face when she turned around. Ishmael stood leaning against a silver Passat. He waved and Nina waved back. Ishmael walked over.

He was smiling. "I think your feet are hurting, am I right?"

Nina grimaced. She didn't answer.

"Come on, ain't you tired of being mad at me yet?"

Nina shook her head, no. "I'm not mad, I'm just disappointed, that's all."

"About what?" Ishmael asked. He was so glad to hear her say more than two words to him. He had finally figured out that Nina might talk to him, if he caught her away from the shop. She had too much pride to entertain his conversation in a room full of women he had already slept with. She looked so pretty, but her face was fixed in agony. Nina shifted her body weight to her other foot to alleviate the pain she was feeling in the toe of her shoes. She hated walking.

Nina tilted her head and looked Ishmael in the eyes. "I liked you, Ishmael, and I thought you had potential. Not that I wanted you to be my man." Nina did, but she didn't need to tell him that. "But, I just wanted to see where things would go, and then you fucked it up. I never thought you would run through the whole clique." Nina shook her head. "Now, you got everybody fighting all because you couldn't keep your dick in your pants."

Ishmael nodded. He understood. He had played himself. Trying to be 'the man' had cost him the pleasure of Nina's company. He proceeded with the next step in his plan. "So, I want to make it up to you."

Nina looked skeptical and one of her eyes narrowed in suspicion. "How?"

"I know you don't want to ride in my truck since what happened with Robin, and I don't like you riding home with that dude who works across the street from you." Ishmael waited for Nina to catch on, but she stood waiting for him to continue. Rather than explain, he turned and pointed towards the Passat.

"You're giving me a car? Or, are you putting me on an IOU like you did with Charly?" Nina asked. She silently drooled at the car, instantly in love with it, but she refused to give Ishmael the satisfaction of knowing it.

"Nah, it's all yours. All you have to do is agree to give me another chance." It wasn't much of a sacrifice for Ishmael to give her the car. He had just taken it back from a chick he was no longer dealing with. He got cars all the time, since he was in cahoots with a dealer in Queens. But he didn't tell Nina that. He allowed her to think that he had done this on his own.

Nina looked at Ishmael. "No." She turned for her door, but Ishmael stopped her.

"Come on, baby girl. Don't be like that. I'm not asking you to marry me. Just stop avoiding me like I got the monster."

Nina wouldn't be won over by smooth talk. "I'm avoiding you because you bring too much drama. You're a nice guy, Ish. You're fly, you got style and women love you, but you already know that. I'm not trying to waste my time with somebody who just wants to get another notch on his belt. Sorry."

Nina walked inside and Ishmael was left standing alone again. He looked around to make sure that no one had seen Nina dis him like she did. Then, Ishmael swallowed his pride and went home.

The next morning, Nina walked out her front door only to find that the beautiful silver car was still parked at the curb. She shook her head at Ishmael's persistence, and walked over to the Volkswagen. As she got closer, she saw an envelope stuck under the windshield wiper. When she looked closer, she saw her name scrawled across it and couldn't help but smile. Ishmael was too much!

She picked up the envelope and opened it. Inside was a note written in blue ink. *It's your car, Nina. You shouldn't have to depend on anybody for anything. I just want you to have your own something special. Stop being stubborn.*

Nina couldn't help but smile. She started to fold the note and put it back in its envelope, but she noticed a short sentence written at the bottom of the page. *The key is in your mailbox.*

Nina looked up at the sky and wished her mother was still alive, so that she could tell her about the guy who was winning her over.

The Green Eyed Monster

Nina pulled up in front of *Dime Piece* and parked her car. She fed the meter and walked towards the shop, where Robin was standing outside talking to Charly, of all people. She instantly wondered why Robin was associating with Charly. Nina was in no mood for Charly that day, so she said hello to the both of them, and continued past. She knew that Charly would never dream of following her inside, since Celeste would spazz if she caught her back in the shop. Robin stopped Nina, though.

"Who's car are you driving, Nina? That shit is hot!" Charly stared at the silver four-door vehicle like it was the most beautiful automobile she'd seen. Robin was smiling waiting for Nina to answer her question.

"It's mine," Nina said. She turned to walk away again.

"When did you buy a car?" Charly asked. She knew Nina didn't have the money to afford a 2000 Passat.

Before Nina could answer, a voice behind her did the honors. "I bought it for her."

Nina turned around, and saw Ishmael standing there, looking thrilled to see that she had accepted his gift. Nina frowned, angry that Ishmael had revealed the truth.

Charly glared at Ishmael and folded her arms across her chest. "What?"

Nina also scowled at Ishmael. She didn't need the drama with Charly, and she still had to work with Robin. Knowing that Ishmael had sex with both of them, Nina knew this wasn't going to end calmly. "Where did you come from?" Nina asked. "You just appeared out of nowhere, answering questions that nobody asked you."

Robin stared at Ishmael, looking hurt and confused. Her nineteen years of life experience had not prepared her to deal with a player of Ishmael's caliber. Ishmael was the type who spent money on women whose company he enjoyed. He liked Robin, but in his eyes she was a freak he twisted out on a summer afternoon. He never would have thought of buying her a car or lavishing her with diamond earrings. It wasn't like that with them. Robin was upset, though she tried not to show it.

"I said I bought it for her, Charly. Is there a problem?" Ishmael was challenging her. Charly knew that there was nothing going on between she and him, and it bothered her. She also knew that her actions with Celeste had enraged him. He wanted her to flip out about Nina's car so that he could put her in her place once and for all. "You and I don't deal with each other no more, so don't start getting dramatic."

Charly looked at him long and hard. She looked at Nina. "So, you're fucking with Ishmael now, Nina?"

Nina shook her head. "No, Charly, I don't fuck with Ishmael. We're friends."

"Friends?" Robin laughed. "Ishmael, you have some interesting 'friends'. First, Celeste and now Nina. You sure are good to your 'friends'."

Nina glowered at Ishmael and shook her head. "See what you started?"

Ishmael stood his ground. "I'm glad this is happening. It's time we put all this shit out on the table. Robin we had sex, nothing more."

Charly looked shocked. "You fucked him, too???" Charly's voice was bellowing. She couldn't believe it. Here she was telling Robin how good Ishmael's sex was and all the while Robin was fucking him!

Ishmael wasn't done. He glared at Charly. "And you need to stop questioning muthafuckas about what we do together. I'm not your man, Charly."

"I never said you was, Ishmael. I just think it's fucked up that you would deal with two friends of mine."

"Since when am I a friend of yours, Charly? Since when?" Nina demanded.

Charly didn't answer, but Robin stepped in. "You know you're wrong, Ishmael." Robin's unspoken words were understood by all. Robin felt like she had been used and she was angry.

"I'm not wrong. Everybody here is grown." He explained. "If I fucked you, or you for that matter." Ishmael pointed to Robin. "We both went into it knowing what we were doing. When I make somebody wifey, you'll know it. Until then, what I do is my business." He looked at Nina.

"Can I talk to you in private?" He asked.

Nina considered it and then nodded. The two of them walked off together, with Robin and Charly standing still shooting daggers in their direction.

They walked to the corner where Ishmael's truck was parked. "I know you didn't want me to do that" He said. "But I needed to get that shit off my chest. Now, there ain't no more confusion about who I'm coming to see when I stop by *Dime Piece*. I'm coming for you, Nina."

She looked in his eyes searching for the truth. "Ishmael, you are the biggest player."

"I know that, I can't change the past, but I'm growing up, knawmean? When I fucked Charly, it was because she's a pretty girl. She got a nice body, and I'm a man, that was all a game for me. Robin – I regret doing that, but she was more aggressive about it than I was. That shit just happened.

I guess I was testing the waters, trying to see how far I could go, what I could get away with." Ishmael paused. "But there's something different about you." He kissed Nina on the cheek. "I like you, Nina. I'm not saying that I'm gonna be a saint. I ain't trying to lie to you and make you think I'm on it like that. But, I do like you, and it would be nice to see if it could go somewhere. That's all I'm saying."

"So, what about all the other bitches in your life?"

"What about all the niggas in yours?"

Nina laughed. She wasn't seeing anyone seriously, but she did have a few friends with benefits.

Ishmael continued. "I'm not saying we gotta move too fast and settle down until we know what's gonna happen with us. But, I promise you, that I ain't trying to hurt you, ma. I'm through playing games and I won't embarrass you by fucking your friends and co-workers."

She hit him playfully on the arm and smiled. "I'll just fuck a few of yours if you do."

Ishmael chuckled and nodded his head. "Yeah, I ain't trying to hear no shit like that happening." He looked at her pretty face and asked, "Can I have a real kiss now?"

Nina obliged, and kissed Ishmael right there in broad daylight. And, for the first time, she didn't give a damn who knew, who saw, or who didn't like it. She had one life to live and she was going to live it to the fullest.

Making Love For The First Time

Nina returned to the shop and got through the day as best she could. She managed to finish her clients, while avoiding the stares from her co-workers. In a way, Nina felt vindicated. She had come out on top as far as she was concerned. Charly had been the bragging type. She was the show off, always putting Nina down. But now the script had been flipped and Nina was getting the man. Go figure. Even Robin had come out of the situation a loser. Nina wondered if she was even doing better than Celeste. Celeste, after all, was nothing more than Rah-Lo's mistress. Nina was on the road to being Ishmael's number one, and that was better than anything Celeste had. Nina finished her last client and went home, happy to be free of the tension. When she arrived at her doorstep, Ishmael stood leaning against the door. He looked yummy in a blue Yankee fitted cap, jeans and a throwback jersey. Nina glided over in a pair of small shorts, with a spaghetti strapped top that left little to the imagination. She was a sight for sore eyes.

"Hi." She said, in a soft voice. She couldn't help but smile. She was so happy to see him standing there.

He returned the gesture and said, jokingly, "I was just in the neighborhood and decided to stop by."

Nina led him inside and quipped, "It's so funny how you've committed everyone's address to memory, yet no one ever gets invited to your house."

Ishmael ignored the remark, and looked around the apartment he had only been in once before. Nina put her purse on the table and Ishmael said, "Can I have a tour, please? The last time I was here, you made me stay in the living room. I want to see the rest of the place."

Nina obliged. She showed him her modest, but functional kitchen. Then the bathroom, a large room with an old fashioned bathtub in the middle of the room sitting on four legs. The room was elegant and feminine just like Nina.

Finally, she led him to a door and paused. "I think this is what you want to see." She led him inside to a room that just came together perfectly. She had a leather sleigh bed that sat in the middle of the floor. Her windows were draped in sheer curtains and artwork adorned the walls. She had a real nice flair for decorating, but the room looked lived in. Nina sat on her bed and Ishmael looked around.

"This is really nice." He said. "You had me sittin' on that hard couch all night that time, when you had a room this nice I could have got comfortable in?"

Nina laughed. "My couch is not hard!" She protested. She invited him to sit beside her and he did. He took her hand in his, and examined her long, slender fingers. He noticed that her nails were perfectly manicured and they were soft. He liked that.

"What are you, a palm reader?" she asked, cynically.

"Nah, but I think I know what might happen in the near future."

"What's that?"

"I think you might learn to deal with women who hate on you, because I like spending time with you. I think I'll learn to deal with the fact that when you shut down, you're *impossible*. I think we might enjoy each other's company for a long time."

Nina said nothing. But inside, she wanted everything he had just said to come to pass. He then kissed her. His rhythm was erotically slow and sensual, and Nina felt her nipples react instantaneously. Ishmael held her face lightly in his hands and tongued her ever so softly. She didn't resist when his hands slid down to her shoulders, and he slid her top down to her navel. She felt so vulnerable as he stroked her so softly. Nina reached and pulled at his jersey. His body was perfect, and she wanted to start clapping. He laid her on her back and slid her shorts off. She spread herself for Ishmael and he licked her from head to toe, concentrating his oral skills on the one part she needed them most. Nina came viciously and she hungered for Ishmael. He slid a condom on and took his time with her. He stroked her deeply, slowly and he talked to her erotically. Nina didn't hold back. She gave it up to Ishmael with all that she had, and he felt her fully. He made love to her, and wondered if he had ever made love like that before. Nina drew him in.

Afterwards, she lay on his arm staring at the ceiling. "I'm trying to think of the right thing to say," Ishmael admitted.

Nina smiled. "Finally, you're speechless. You're cute when you're speechless."

Ishmael slept the night away with Nina in his arms. When he woke up beside her in the morning, she looked just as good as she had in his dreams.

All Falls Down

Nina parked her car outside *Dime Piece* the next morning. She was still flying high from being with Ishmael. He had made love to her again in the morning when they woke up. Then they ate breakfast in their underwear and showered together. He had left her with a long kiss goodbye, and a smile on her face. As she walked towards the shop, she saw the sun shining, felt a breeze blowing and she could have sworn she heard harps playing in heaven.

But, as soon as she walked in the salon, she knew she was in Brooklyn. There was a vendor selling mixtapes and bootleg cd's, and a conversation was going on about Rikki Lake. Nina noticed Robin and Celeste in the back talking quietly. When they saw Nina, they separated and went back to work. Celeste breezed past Nina.

"You're late." She hissed.

Nina was surprised. She was never late, so why was Celeste making a big deal about one time? Nina shrugged it off thinking, Celeste must be feeling the pressure of having to take more clients since Charly's absence. "Sorry." She said.

They got through the morning easily since the customers were steady. They were all busy until mid afternoon. Robin went out to get something to eat, and came back with Charly following behind. Celeste immediately began to flip as soon as she saw them approaching the shop. Charly knew better than to step foot inside of Celeste's domain. So, while Charly waited outside, Robin entered *Dime Piece* and was met with an onslaught from Celeste. Celeste began questioning immediately. "What the hell did you bring her around here for?"

"She just wants to talk to Nina." Robin explained.

No one was more surprised than Nina. She walked right outside with her apron on and a comb in her hand.

"Yes?" she asked, facing Charly.

"Nina, Ishmael spent the night with you?"

Nina laughed. "Damn, Charly. Let me find out he needs to get a restraining order against you. You stalking him now?"

"I passed your house on my way to work, and saw his car outside. Just come clean and tell the truth. You livin' foul!"

"Bitch, please!" Nina turned to walk back in the shop, but Charly hog spit at her, and a large wad of phlegm landed in Nina's long, lovely hair. Nina turned so fast with her hands fisted, that she caught Robin on the chin accidentally. Robin came right back and hit Nina as hard as she could. The shop spilled out, and Charly held the spectators at bay yelling, "Let them fight! Let them fight!" Celeste pushed Charly out of the way and separated the women, chastising them.

"You're a mother, Robin. Now, you're out here fighting in the street like a little girl!" Celeste turned to Nina. "You out here fighting over what Nina, a guy?"

"This ain't got nothing to do with that."

"That's what you think!" Celeste looked at the whole picture. She looked at Charly. "Get the fuck away from my shop before I use the gift Rah-Lo gave me." Celeste would have loved to shoot Charly.

They all went back inside, leaving Charly to mumble under her breath. Once inside, Celeste summoned both women to her office.

"You two can't be doing this shit, I don't want my shop associated with all this bullshit."

Nina stood silent, while Robin tried to explain. "She hit me. What was I supposed to do?"

"Robin, since when do you hang out with Charly?" Celeste interrupted. "When she was here, you were at each other's throat. Now, Nina's dealing with Ishmael, and you and Charly are best friends. What's up with that?'

Robin had no answer. Celeste looked at Nina. "Robin, give me a minute alone with Nina."

Robin left, closing the door behind her. Celeste wasted no time. "I'm hearing some things, Nina."

"What kind of things?"

"Are you really fucking with Ishmael, knowing that he slept with Charly and Robin?"

"Ishmael slept with more women than just Charly and Robin."

"But you don't work with those women, you work with us. So, am I supposed to keep losing stylists because of you, Nina?"

Nina stood amazed. "Celeste, Charly left because you beat her ass, not because I was dealing with Ishmael. Robin has to get over it, it's as simple as that."

"Ishmael doesn't love you, Nina." Celeste knew when she said it, that it had nothing to do with business anymore. Her anger with Nina had more to do with the fact that she was winning Ishmael's heart, than with anything work related.

"He doesn't love you either, Celeste." Nina looked at Celeste, deadpanned. "But Rah-Lo does, and that's all you need to worry about."

"Careful, Nina. You could get fired talking to me like that. Don't bite the hand that feeds you, sweetie." Celeste's tone was condescending.

Nina smirked. "I've been feeding myself with my own hand for far too long to let you intimidate me, Celeste. I quit."

Nina walked out of Celeste's office, and out of the shop. She never looked back.

Happily Ever After?

Rah-Lo turned the key in the door. He crept up the stairs to their bedroom, where he found Celeste sleeping peacefully in the king sized bed. He slid in beside her and she woke up, ecstatic that he had come home unannounced. She couldn't believe he had surprised her. Asia had picked him up and brought him home two days prior, all without Celeste's knowledge. Rah-Lo had to put in time with his wife and kids before coming to see the woman he loved more than money. Celeste had never been happier. They devoured each other, both of them tired of waiting to feel the other's touch. The sex was intense and it was perfect. They both lay together afterwards, enjoying each other's touch.

Celeste fed him breakfast in bed and spoiled Rah-Lo to the fullest. They spent more time alone together than ever before. It was like old times, and Celeste realized how much she had missed him. Rah-Lo was glad to be back as well. He missed Celeste like crazy, but he was also glad to be home, because he was trying to maintain his hold on the streets. Ishmael had done a good job, but Rah-Lo wanted everyone to know that he was back in town. It wasn't long before he was back in the streets. Ishmael played his position as his right hand man, since their crew had been diminished considerably. J-Shawn was dead, Harry was doing big time, and Pappy was on the run, but living dangerously; tinkering on the edge of life and death. So, Rah-Lo began to rebuild, and Celeste began to withdraw. She was scared of losing Rah-Lo to prison again, but she was even more afraid of losing him to death in the mean streets of Brooklyn.

To add more fuel to the fire, she was feeling the heat of having to replace Charly and Nina. She got a couple of young girls to rent space in the shop. The two had a modest following. They worked hard, but they were not as good as Charly or Nina, they were not even close. Celeste was beginning to feel frustrated and fed up with trying to keep the business afloat. She thumbed through the bills, frustrated beyond words. Somehow the dream had crashed around her. Rah-Lo was never going to change. Celeste was finally able to admit that to herself. She was sick of being Asia's understudy in a drama that was shaping up to have a sad ending. Rah-Lo wasn't leaving his wife. He wasn't leaving the streets. Celeste started to feel as if she had been wasting her time. And she started to look for a way out.

Meanwhile, Nina sat in her apartment, angry and feeling betrayed. Celeste was bad mouthing her to all her clients. Rumors in the hood were swirling about Nina. They were saying Nina stole Charly's man, and that she thought she was better than Celeste. She couldn't believe that the tables had turned, and that this was how things were going down. She was back to square one, looking for a new place to do business, and trying to maintain her existing clientele by making house calls. She was fed up and she felt like she was going in circles. Nina's biggest fear was losing everything she had worked so hard for. She was tired of losing, and sick of being the only one to ever take a loss. It was time to take matters into her own hands. She called Ishmael and asked him to meet her at her house at 10 p.m.

Robin and Charly sat in the West Indian restaurant, discussing the new developments at *Dime Piece*. Charly was glad to hear that Celeste had resorted to hiring mediocre workers. All the clients they lost were coming to Charly. She felt like she had emerged victorious, since she reaped the financial rewards of Celeste's decline in business. But, Charly was still bitter about the fight they'd had. She still had scars from Celeste punching her with rings on. Charly knew for sure that it wasn't over yet. She had more in store for Celeste, a whole lot more.

As she was finishing her beef patty, she saw Ishmael's truck pull up outside and he stepped out to talk to a colleague. Charly quickly discarded what was left of her meal, and rushed outside. She told Robin she'd catch up with her later and she walked over to Ishmael.

"Wassup, Ish?" Charly chewed her gum the whole time. "Long time, no see."

Ishmael gave her a half-smile. "Wassup, Charly. How you doing?"

"Not so good. I don't hear from you anymore. What happened, you forgot about me?"

Ishmael nodded. "Yeah I did." He said, and got back in his truck and started to pull off, but Charly walked over to the window on the driver's side.

"Why you acting like that, Ish. I'm not gonna tell Nina."

Ishmael started the car. "I know, because I won't give you nothing to tell Nina." He pulled off, and Charly was left behind. She nodded and walked away. No more playing fair.

Ishmael arrived back at the place he called home. He entered his apartment in Clinton Hill. He looked around, happy with all the luxuries he had attained for himself. He lived in a spacious home all alone. He never invited women to his house unless they were serious. So far, only two women had achieved that honor. Ishmael was protective of his home and never took unannounced visitors. Few knew where he lived, to begin with. So, the ones he brought there, felt honored to be invited.

For years, he had been content to live alone. He didn't long for the company of a woman often enough to want to sleep and wake up with that person day after day.

But lately, he had begun to feel like he might want that. He started thinking about the cold winter coming up, and how nice it would be to have her in his arms each night to keep him warm. Ishmael had to admit to himself that he had a jones for Nina.

When she called and asked him to meet her at her place that night, Ishmael started getting ready. By 9:30, he had taken a shower, gotten dressed in his cream colored Sean Jean outfit and started out the door.

The phone rang, interrupting his departure. He answered it, and the person on the other end was hysterical. "Celeste? What happened?"

Ishmael couldn't believe his ears. "I'm on my way." He said. He hung up the phone and ran out the door, headed for Lawrence Street.

The Aftermath

Ishmael arrived on the scene at *Dime Piece*, and couldn't believe his eyes. The shop was burnt to the ground. The once beautiful salon was gone. Nothing remained but ashes and rubble as the fire department put out the last of the fire. He made his way through the crowd to Celeste's side. She was watching in tears as the shop went up in smoke.

Celeste shook her head. "They said it was arson. Somebody set my shit on fire, Ishmael." Celeste seemed so upset. She called him after trying to get in touch with Rah-Lo, to no avail. Once again, it was Ishmael who came to her side while Rah-Lo was nowhere in sight. She looked at Ishmael, and he put his arm around her to console her. Ishmael asked her once again, "You still willing to be the second runner up? Where's your man, Celeste?"

She responded in anger. "What the fuck, Ishmael? How you sound right now? We both know that I should walk away. But I can't, Ish. And I can't explain why."

He wanted to say something reassuring, but the words didn't come. He struggled to make her feel better, but his train of thought was cut off by Rah-Lo's presence. Rah-Lo walked up on the scene and saw Ishmael and Celeste. Rah-Lo's gaze immediately fell on Ishmael, who was standing with Celeste in his arms. Ishmael sensed Rah-Lo's displeasure and he removed himself from the embrace.

Celeste, also looked caught out there and she quickly tried to fill the pregnant pause.

"My shop is gone, Rah-Lo. They said somebody burned my shit down." Celeste let a tear fall, and Rah-Lo quickly wiped it away for her.

"Don't cry, mama. You got insurance on this place. You can rebuild it if you want to."

He hugged Celeste and eyed Ishmael. Rah-Lo hoped his friend knew that he loved Celeste and would kill over her, but Rah-Lo felt guilty for having such thoughts. Ishmael was his boy, he wouldn't do that to him. Rah-Lo brushed off his suspicion, as Ishmael gave his condolences for the loss of the salon and said goodbye. Rah-Lo watched Ishmael pull away in his truck, wondering how he could ever doubt a friend as good as that. If only he knew the full extent of that friendship.

Across the street from where Rah-Lo and Celeste stood, Charly smiled a devilish grin. Things couldn't have worked out better.

Nina was worried about Ishmael when he didn't show up at 10pm as planned. By 11:30, her concern had turned to anger. He finally arrived with midnight only minutes away, and Nina didn't hesitate to start the inquisition. "What happened?"

Ishmael explained. "Celeste called me and..."

"Celeste?" Nina's jealousy was evident. "Why couldn't she call Rah-Lo?"

"She couldn't get in touch with him. And she needed somebody to be there because *Dime Piece* burned to the ground."

"It burned down? How?"

"Somebody set it on fire."

Nina frowned. "Celeste probably did it to get the insurance money," she said.

Ishmael also frowned. "Nah, she wouldn't do no shit like that."

Nina hated to hear him defend Celeste. The affection was evident in his tone. But rather than start an argument, she took his hand and led him to the sofa.

"So what did you call me over here for? On the phone, you sounded like you had something important to say." Ishmael asked, not sure if he really wanted to hear the answer.

Nina nodded. What she wanted was to level with Ishmael. "I wanted to tell you about me. I wanted to lay it all out and let you know who I am, and I want you to feel free to do the same. I'm really not for the games anymore. So if you want to spend time with me, you should know all about me." She told him her whole story. She told him about the childhood she had with a single mother on welfare, the sex she had trying to fill up the empty space left by her father's absence. She told Ishmael about the struggle she had to survive on her own at such a young age when her mother died. And Ishmael listened. He also opened up, telling Nina about his own life. The drug infested projects, the sister who was fast and wild and wound up with a psycho. He told her how he got in the game. He even leveled with her about his affection for Celeste. He explained his feelings towards her and his sense of loyalty towards Rah-Lo, and Ishmael laid all his cards out on the table. Him and Nina opened up completely and got naked together both in the physical sense and in the emotional sense for the first time. It was a beautiful thing.

A New Day

Celeste did get the insurance money, just as Rah-Lo told her. But she decided not to reopen the shop. Instead, she started really thinking about the questions Ishmael had asked her. Was she still willing to play second runner up? She was tired of all the whispers and the stares. She was, after all, nothing more than what her mother called a 'kept woman'. Celeste's mother had been lecturing her a lot lately; telling her to consider moving to Atlanta with her and Nana. They had a nice piece of property and the section was an emerging community of new homes and middle class Black folks. Celeste could easily buy a home near her mother and start all over. She didn't shrug it off. Instead, she put that money in the bank, some in savings bonds and began to plan for the day she would leave all the drama behind. She was tired of working with women day in and day out and opted to change to a different way of life. She had enough of the lifestyle she was living. It was time to start a new day.

Ishmael looked over at the sexy woman sitting in the passenger seat and smiled with pride. Nina looked like a goddess with her hair pinned up and her delicate neckline exposed. Nina still had no idea where they were going, all she knew was that Ishmael said it was a surprise. She hadn't had one of those in a long time.

"At least tell me half of the surprise." She coaxed him.

"Nope, you have to wait till we get there." Ishmael turned the radio up to drown out her questions. Nina laughed at his actions, and looked out the window as they passed Charly's new shop. The big awning outside read *CHARLY'S,* and Nina couldn't help scowling in contempt. Ishmael noticed, but said nothing. Charly's place had recently opened. She even hired Robin as the braider. Three months had passed since the fire had destroyed *Dime Piece.* Everyone seemed to be moving on, and Ishmael was happy about that. But, now it was time for him to get on with his own life.

He drove another few blocks and pulled up at the curb outside of a residential walk up. "What is this?"

Ishmael smiled. "This is my place. I live here."

Nina smiled. She had finally been invited to the "bat cave". She knew that this meant something special, since Ishmael spent most of his time at her house. He had never invited her to his own until now. "Come on, let's go inside." She said.

Ishmael shook his head. "Wait a minute." He said. "This is only half the surprise." He smiled at her, as she sat waiting for him to finish. "I want you to think about coming to live with me. Let me see if you could have my last name someday."

Nina was floored. "Really?"

He nodded. "Yeah, if you want to."

Nina did want to, more than anything. She kissed Ishmael, and said the words she'd been avoiding for far too long. "I love you."

Ishmael smiled, realizing he had walked away with the real dime piece. "I love you, too." He said. He felt so comfortable saying those words, having let go of his longing for Celeste. He knew she would never leave Rah-Lo. Ishmael was convinced that she would never walk away from her relationship. And he was done waiting in vain.

They headed inside to the place they would call home together. Nina wondered why she'd ever been jealous of any other woman. That was wasted energy. It had all worked out in the end. She held Ishmael's hand, as they walked side by side, into the first day of the rest of their lives.

Epilogue

When the flight landed in Atlanta, Celeste stepped off the plane and walked to the baggage claim area. She waited until she saw her luggage coming down the conveyor belt. After retrieving it, she dialed a number on her cell phone to find out where her ride was at. She wondered for a fleeting moment if she had done the right thing. Walking away from Rah-Lo and Ishmael – two men that she knew loved her genuinely – that scared her most of all. Before she could finish dialing, a familiar voice behind her caused her heart to race in excitement.

"Give your mama some sugar, girl. I'm so happy to see you."

Celeste turned around and embraced her mother. She hugged her tightly, for all the years she had been too hardheaded to do it. Her mother returned the embrace, stroking her daughter's back, lovingly. "Come on. Let's get you home so you can eat something."

Celeste followed her mother out to the car, smiling all the while. She knew she had made the right decision. Her mother and grandmother had fallen in love with the city, and Celeste was anxious to try it out as well. Celeste's mother had suggested that she buy a house on the same residential block in the prestigious Buckhead section and start fresh. After considering it for what seemed like ages, Celeste decided it was a good move for her to make. She didn't tell

Rah-Lo. Instead, she left in the wee hours of the morning, while he was at home with his wife and kids, and headed for Newark airport. She knew that if she told Rah-Lo, he would try to stop her, promising her that he would leave Asia when the time was right. He would leave when his daughters were old enough to understand. Celeste had enough of empty promises. She needed guarantees.

She wrote Rah-Lo a letter and left it in his now empty home on Howard Avenue. She had all of her belongings sent to her mother's home via a moving and storage company and she knew the emptiness of the place she and Rah-Lo had called home for so long would hit him like a ton of bricks.

When Rah-Lo did find the letter, he was devastated. He sat in the kitchen of the empty home, amazed that Celeste would leave him like this. He read her letter.

Raheem,

I love you so much. I always have and always will. But I can't live like this anymore. Life is short, and I don't want to look back on mine with any regrets. I don't wish I had done anything differently. Everything in life is a lesson. You taught me so much and I want you to know that the love I have for you can never be replaced or duplicated. But it's time for me to move on and start treating myself the way I deserve to be treated.

I want to get my own mansion, my own diamonds and furs, put my self through college. I wan to start a new business for myself. I wish you and Asia all the best and hope that you forgive me for walking away. I had no choice. I was suffocating.

I will never stop loving you. Never.
Celeste.

Rah-Lo sat with his head in his hands, tears in his eyes, and a million regrets washing over him. He missed her already and knew that he would never find another love like the one that they shared. He wanted her back so badly that he wondered how he could get by without her in his life.

Harry wound up doing ten years in prison. He was released and rearrested in the same year. He's now serving the rest of his twenty-five year sentence. Pappy was found dead on the roof of a building in Brooklyn's Farragut projects. He was shot between the eyes and the case was never solved.

Charly and Robin became tight like Cagney and Lacey. The two ran the shop successfully, and kept the clients updated on all the latest gossip. Charly began dating Neo, the archrival of Ishmael and Rah-Lo, but she never admitted any involvement in *Dime Piece*'s demise. Many suspect that she lit the match that brought it crumbling down. Others think Celeste was cunning and smart enough to realize that business was slow and the bills were still pouring in. They suspected she torched the salon to collect the windfall. Or had Asia gotten tired of Rah-Lo and his mistress once an for all? Some mysteries will never be solved.

Robin continued to raise her son as a single mother, trying to find time for herself, as well. She got over Ishmael, Charly never did.

Ishmael and Nina were still going strong. The two of them continued to take their love one day at a time, allowing all the pieces to fall into place as they should. Ishmael was stunned when he learned that Celeste had left Rah-Lo and never looked back. In his heart, she would always be the woman he loved first. In the back of his mind, he wondered if sparks would reignite should their paths ever cross again. But he reminded himself that he couldn't concern himself with wondering. He had a sure thing with Nina.

On their one-year anniversary as a couple, Ishmael purchased a salon for Nina one block away from *Charly's*.

She called it **Nappy Nina's**, and she was their toughest competition. The rivalry continues.

THE END

ORDER FORM

Triple Crown Publications
2959 Stelzer Rd.
Columbus, Oh 43219

Name: _____

Address: _____

City/State: _____

Zip: _____

		TITLES	PRICES
		Dime Piece	$15.00
		Gangsta	$15.00
		Let That Be The Reason	$15.00
		A Hustler's Wife	$15.00
		The Game	$15.00
		Black	$15.00
		Dollar Bill	$15.00
		A Project Chick	$15.00
		Road Dawgz	$15.00
		Blinded	$15.00
		Diva	$15.00
		Sheisty	$15.00
		Grimey	$15.00
		Me & My Boyfriend	$15.00
		Larceny	$15.00
		Rage Times Fury	$15.00
		A Hood Legend	$15.00
		Flipside of The Game	$15.00
		Menage's Way	$15.00

SHIPPING/HANDLING (Via U.S. Media Mail)   **$3.95**

TOTAL   **$_____**

FORMS OF ACCEPTED PAYMENTS:

Postage Stamps, Institutional Checks & Money Orders, all mail in orders take 5-7 Business days to be delivered.

ORDER FORM

Triple Crown Publications
2959 Stelzer Rd.
Columbus, Oh 43219

Name: _____

Address: _____

City/State: _____

Zip: _____

	TITLES	PRICES
	Still Sheisty	$15.00
	Chyna Black	$15.00
	Game Over	$15.00
	Cash Money	$15.00
	Crack Head	$15.00
	For the Strength of You	$15.00
	Down Chick	$15.00
	Dirty South	$15.00
	Cream	$15.00
	Hood Winked	$15.00
	Bitch	$15.00
	Stacy	$15.00
	Life Wtihout Hope	$15.00

SHIPPING/HANDLING (Via U.S. Media Mail)   **$3.95**

TOTAL $_____

FORMS OF ACCEPTED PAYMENTS:

Postage Stamps, Institutional Checks & Money Orders, all mail in orders take 5-7 Business days to be delivered.